SAVAGE DADDY

BOSTON MAFIA DONS

BIANCA COLE

CONTENTS

SCARLETT

I step into the dimly lit room of the shady club.

My heart is pounding hard and fast, making me feel sick. The organizers have set up a stage in the center of the room with a stool and microphone on it and nothing else.

I've been on stage since I was little. Dancing is my passion, but it's one of the hardest professions to make money in. The money I desperately need to help my mother. When I saw the advert online to sell your virginity to the highest bidder, I thought it was a joke. Until I found out that it's a thing, not legal, but it happens in places like this.

A few other anxious-looking girls are standing to one side, glancing around the room. None of the buyers are here yet. It's a strange sensation being in a room where everyone knows the embarrassing truth. All the girls here, including me, are virgins.

A man with a clipboard approaches. "Name?"

"Scarlett Carmichael." I twist my fingers together nervously, wondering if I'm making a huge mistake.

There's no denying that I'm desperate for the cash and have no other way of getting it. It's a life-or-death situation. Surely, selling your virginity can't be that terrible. At least, that's what I've been telling myself.

This place will be crawling with the creepiest men imaginable. I repeat the same thing over and over, trying to convince myself it will be fine.

It's only one night.

"Come with me, please," the man says.

I follow him toward the back of the club, noticing that they dressed all the women already here in the same skimpy, sheer, white dress that leaves nothing to the imagination. A shudder races down my spine at the thought of wearing that in front of anyone.

The man leads me into a room at the back. Three other women are stripping and dressing into the same sheer dresses.

He turns around and passes me one. "Strip and put this on." His eyes drag down my body slowly. "No underwear beneath, and then come out to stand with the rest of the girls in the club for now."

I swallow hard and take the dress. The other girls all look as terrified as me. No one is speaking as we all strip together in the small room and put on the dress that ensures the assets we're selling are on display.

My stomach churns, and I can hear my best friend, Kaia, warning me not to do this. She would have thought I was insane if I'd suggested it to her, but I won't stand by while my mother can't pay for her medical bills. I've got something to sell that will save her life and no other way of getting the money. There was no question about doing this for her after everything she's done for me. If she knew, though, she would kill me.

The man that showed me in here claps his hands behind me, making me jump. "I need all of you out of here quickly. Lots of girls are waiting to dress."

There must be at least twenty women, if not more. It's hard to believe that there is such a market for a woman's virginity. Quickly, I slide the sheer dress over my head and place my clothes in my bag. I fold my arms over my chest, before walking back into the club.

I always refused dates with guys as I was too busy practicing dance, hoping to make it big. It's one reason I'm still a virgin at twenty-four years old, but not the main one.

I'm struggling to make ends meet and can't afford my mother's medical bills since the doctors diagnosed her with breast cancer a month ago. She took out a high-interest loan to cover the initial costs, but repayments start soon and neither of us has the money to cover it.

I'm hoping my virginity will sell for enough to clear the debt entirely and pay for more treatment. I've heard that auctions often fetch two-hundred and fifty thousand dollars, which is insane.

The man who ushered me into the changing rooms now stands on a large stage in the center of the room, holding a microphone. "Girls, can I have your attention please," he says.

The limited chatter in the room stops, and everyone looks at him.

"Thank you." He clears his throat. "I want to explain what happens at the auction. One by one, I will call you up onto the stage so the buyers can see what is on offer. You each have a number sewn into the left corner of your dresses, and this is the number that we will call."

I glance down and see my number is twenty-three. A lot of the surrounding girls do the same.

"Once all the girls have been onto the stage, the bidding will start in order. You will wait in these holding chairs until the bidding on your number is complete." He signals to a brightly lit seating area in front of the stage. "Then you'll follow Aleks here to the back room, where the buyer will collect you. We already have your bank details, and we will wire your eighty percent share of the auction price to you instantly."

The guy isn't American. He has an eastern European accent. I wonder what kind of criminal ring is behind this event. The thought makes my stomach churn, as the last thing I want is to get on the wrong side of the law for this.

A pretty girl leans toward me. "Are you as nervous as I am?"

I shrug. "Pretty nervous." I can't deal with small talk right now. My mind is far too distracted. Thankfully, before she can say another word, we're ushered behind the curtains of the stage.

"Now, the buyers will enter the room, and I want all of you to organize yourselves in your number order in a line," Aleks orders.

I wait as chaos ensues, knowing there's no point trying to find my space until there's order. Once most girls have gotten into the right order, I find my spot. The girl next to me looks more nervous than I feel.

Time is moving at a snail's pace as we wait, listening to the announcer address the men ready to bid on us. From the look on the other women's faces around me, they're all as nervous about this as I am.

The two girls ahead of me speak to each other in hushed tones, but I can hear them. "Do you think the men that are going to bid are dangerous?" Number twenty-two asks.

Number twenty-one shakes her head. "I doubt it. They're probably a load of horny old men that want to deflower young women."

The girl next to me wrinkles her nose. "God, I hope they aren't too old."

I sigh heavily, trying to ignore their pointless conversation. Did they expect to get paid for their virginity and enjoy the process?

It's highly unlikely that this auction draws a load of hot young men ready to bid on us. The guys out there will be the kind that you don't want to meet. They'll be dark and twisted and more than likely older than any of us.

All that matters is getting the money to pay for my mom's care. If the guy I must lose my virginity to is eighty years old, then so be it. I'd do it one-hundred times over to save her life. I can't sit back and do nothing while she suffers.

Aleks returns backstage, clapping his hands. "No chitchat. This isn't a get-together. I want all of you to focus and listen for your numbers. Do you understand?"

There's silence across the room as everyone stares blankly at him.

"I said, do you understand?" he growls, making a few of the girls jump.

"Yes," we all say in chorus. It feels like I'm back in high school. Something tells me that getting on the wrong side of Aleks, or any of the organizers here, would result in a worse punishment than detention. These men aren't lawful. This auction isn't lawful.

I may only be twenty-four years old, but I've never done something illegal before. It makes my stomach twist to think that I could effectively go to jail for this.

Then who would look after my mom?

It's just one night.

I repeat my calming mantra in my mind, hoping that I don't end up having a panic attack. The chances of the police showing up and shutting this down are slim. The setup seems sophisticated, and these guys appear to be professionals.

One night and I'll be able to pay off my mom's loan and make the payments for the rest of her treatment. I know that taking this risk is worth it. All I can hope is that the man that buys my virginity isn't a psychopath.

"Thank you for coming to the virgin auction. Now that we've been through the process, we will start," I hear the guy in charge speak over the microphone.

My heart skips a beat as this is happening. There's no turning back now. I'm about to sell myself to the highest bidder.

2

MALACHY

"*B*oss, the car is ready for you," Niall says, interrupting my work.

I meet his gaze and nod. "Thanks, lad." I log out of my computer, shutting it down before heading out of my office. "Are you sure you don't want to come with me for the fun of it?"

Niall meets my gaze, shaking his head. "Nah, buying women isn't my style."

I laugh. "You don't know what you're missing." I clap him on the back. "Women that are bought can be used in any way you want." I wink at Niall. My tastes with women are so rough and twisted that I have a hard time finding one that's willing to sleep with me.

The unsuspecting virgins at the auctions are always the best, as they're ruined once I finally set them free. None of them expect that selling their virginity means sleeping with me until I'm bored with them. The boredom normally hits me fast once I've broken a woman's resolve. I don't pay over a million dollars for one fuck.

"I'm sure they are." He laughs. "I heard what happened at the docks yesterday. Do we have a retaliation in mind for the Italians?"

I run a hand across my beard, shaking my head. "Not yet. We'll have a sit down with the guys in the next couple of days to put in place a plan of action." I shrug. "The truth of it is we're at war, and there will be no ending it soon."

"Aye, I expected as much," Niall says, patting me on the shoulder. "Shall I set up the sit down for the day after tomorrow?"

I nod in response. "Sounds good, lad. See you later." I walk out of the office and head toward the front door, noticing my sister Alicia lingering to one side.

"What are you doing, Sis?"

She shrugs. "Are you going to one of those terrible auctions again?"

I clench my jaw, knowing that Alicia can't accept my ways. Despite my attempts to shield my baby sister from my depravity, I've failed. All she wants is for me to find a lovely girl and settle down with a family, which is not in the cards for me. I'm too broken in ways she could never understand. Alicia is my half-sister and was born five years after me. We've been through hell and back together, but I've always protected her, no matter what.

"What does it matter?" I ask.

Alicia sighs heavily. "Why don't you give my friend Jane a chance and go on one date?"

Because Jane would go running the other way once she knew my tastes in the bedroom; I don't do gentle. I hardly know the meaning of the word. "Believe me, little sis. Your friend wants nothing to do with me." I kiss my sister on the cheek. "Don't wait up." I walk away before she can further protest about my decision to buy another woman.

Niall parked my Chevy Impala out front for me. I slide into the driver's seat. Ever since that bastard, Milo, blew up my corvette, I've been angrier than normal. It's bubbling under the surface, and it will be until I get my revenge on him.

Wars aren't ideal. I wanted to avoid it, but when he killed my cousin, Sean, there was no option. Even if Sean was a fucking two-faced son of a bitch working for the Russians. The only people I hate more than the Italians are the Russians.

I turn over the engine and put it into gear before driving toward the electric gates. They open once they sense the car. Four of my men stand guard at the gates, and they give me a nod as I pass. I don't normally have so many men on my grounds, but with the war looming, it's necessary.

My cell phone rings as I turn onto the main road toward the club. It's Aiden, one of my men. I take the call on hands-free.

"What is it?" I ask.

"It's the information on Mikhail Gurin."

I clench my jaw, knowing that this isn't the right time to hear the news. If that Italian son of a bitch Milo Mazzeo is right, my cousin Sean fucked me over. "What have you learned?"

"It's true that Sean was working for him, stealing shipments from the Italians."

My hands clench the steering wheel so hard I might tear it off. "How long?"

Aiden clears his throat. "Six months, we think. He started small, but it was only a matter of time until the Italians caught them."

"That bloody idiot," I growl, punching the dashboard. "You can bring me the evidence at the sit down the day after tomorrow. Niall is arranging everything."

"Aye, boss."

I cancel the call and focus my attention on the road. Rage coils through me that my flesh and blood would betray me like that. The one thing that is more important to me than anything is family, and I'm loyal to a fault. I shouldn't have started this war if Sean crossed me like that. If he was stealing Italian drugs, he should have stolen them for us, not the Russians.

Milo was justified in killing him, but he should have given me the privilege. Family may be important to me, but I won't tolerate a rat even if he is my blood relation.

The club car park is packed as a lot of the regulars enter the building. The girls lately at this auction have been predictable and a little boring, crying too fucking much for my liking. I need to pick a tougher girl tonight, especially if I want to get my money's worth.

I park in my usual reserved spot and turn off the engine. It's been a good few months since the last auction, and the last woman only lasted a week before she was a useless, sniveling mess.

I step out of the car and shut the door, locking my car. Someone clears their throat behind me to get my attention. I turn around and see Jameson, a sleazy politician who is always at these events. He doesn't always bid but comes along for the show more than half the time.

"Jameson, what can I do for you?" I ask, wondering why this asshole would approach me before I've got a drink in my hand.

He shakes his head. "I heard you are having issues with Milo Mazzeo. It's what I can do for you."

I hold my hand up to stop him. "If you want to talk business, then call my secretary. I'm not working right now."

He looks a little irritated by my refusal to talk about Milo. He's never liked him and is one of the few politicians who understands Boston's criminal underworld. "Fine. I'll call her."

I turn my back on him and take a step away.

"I could help you bring him down, but it won't be cheap, especially since you can't even give me the time of day."

I smirk at his stupid, self-important comment, which

he'll regret. "I'll pay whatever the fuck I want, Jameson. Or I'll walk away. Do you think I need your help with the Italians?" I don't glance back at him.

"No, but you could show me some more respect when I'm trying to help."

I turn around slowly and narrow my eyes at him. The stare I give him makes him pale. It's enough to make most men pale, but this guy is a fucking sissy. "Do you know who you are talking to, lad? I wouldn't push me if I were you unless you want a broken nose." I clench my fists by my side. No one demands respect from me, especially not a cowardly politician like him.

He holds his hands up in surrender. "Of course, I apologize. I'll call your secretary."

I grunt in response and turn my back on him, marching into the club. It feels like everything leading up to this auction is designed to piss me off. It doesn't bode well for my purchase tonight.

When I'm angry, I like to take it out on an unsuspecting little virgin. The place is busy, and it won't be long until the show starts. I swear some perverts here come for the show and never buy.

I take my seat at my regular table at the front and lean back, surveying the men here tonight. Jameson sneaks in and takes his seat opposite me at the same table, keeping his gaze down.

He's clever not to speak to me again. If he thinks his position on the city council somehow makes him untouchable, he's wrong. I won't hesitate to kill men that cross me, no matter who they are.

I glance behind me and see Mikhail is attending this auction and is at the VIP table on the club's mezzanine. The pakhan of the Russian mafia in Boston. He never buys, only comes now and then to watch his own auction. The guy is more private than I am, and that's saying something.

The background music starts, and I turn my attention to the stage where one of Mikhail's men is standing in front of the microphone. "Thank you for coming to the virgin auction," he says before reeling off the usual instructions for bidding, which I don't listen to. I've been here enough times to know how it works.

I tap my fingers against my table, wishing the server would take my drink order. The whiskey is practically calling me. It's often slow service as Mikhail doesn't employ enough servers for the number of guys that turn up.

Two Russians are sitting at my table. It makes me uneasy as they talk together in their mother tongue. I don't trust the Russians, as they're worse than the Italians. Even after the ordeal that I had with Milo and his wife.

"Can I get you something to drink?" A waitress I've never seen here before asks. She's pretty but looks too young to be working in a club.

I smile at her, but it only seems to make her nervous

as she fiddles with a strand of hair. "Sure, whiskey on the rocks. Make it a double."

She writes my order down on a pad, her hands shaking as she does. Her attention moves to the Russians. "Chto ya mogu zastavit' vas vypit'?" She speaks to them in Russian, making my blood boil.

I need to find a better auction than this, but there isn't one in Boston. The Russians are the best at organizing events like this. "Would you bastards speak English? We're in America, for fuck's sake." I glare at the two men who stop talking and stare at me.

"Russians own this club, so I'd watch your mouth, ty irlandskiy podonok."

I grit my teeth, clenching my fists on the table. Right now, I'm ready to explode and would love to paint this table with this idiot's blood. "What the fuck did you call me?"

The waitress hurries back to our table and sets the glass of whiskey down in front of me. "I'm sorry for the wait, sir." She glances at the two Russians. "Also, Vlad and Igor, can you come with me? Mikhail has requested your presence at his table."

They glare at me before nodding and standing. It looks like Mikhail noticed a fatal mistake that none of his staff did, which was putting Russians on my table.

Jameson clears his throat. "To be honest, their Russian was pissing me off too."

I narrow my eyes at him. "Did I ask your opinion?"

He shakes his head. "No, but I don't see why we

can't get along tonight. I don't intend to discuss business any further."

I take a long, soothing sip of the top-shelf Irish whiskey. The heat of it burning down my throat eases some of my anger. Rage is an emotion that I've struggled to contain for as long as I can remember. It's why I turned to bare-knuckle fighting—an outlet for all the dangerous rage bubbling beneath the surface.

I need to relax and enjoy the show. By the end of the night, I'll have a new plaything to enjoy and take out my frustrations with.

3

SCARLETT

"*N*umber twenty-two," the announcer says over the microphone, making my heart rate accelerate.

The girl next to me walks out of the line, leaving me to go next. I'm shaking with nerves. This is worse than all my dance recitals combined, as I'm naked. The thought of the men out there surveying me like a piece of meat makes my skin crawl.

"Number twenty-three," the voice calls.

I stand frozen and staring at the entrance to the stage. The girl next to me clears her throat. "That's you."

I glance at her, and she gives me a reassuring smile. "It's daunting, but there's no backing out now."

I nod and walk toward the stage, hearing my heart pound in my ears. It's eerily silent in the club except for some faint music playing in the background. The glaring lights make it impossible to see the men I know are lurking in the darkness beyond.

I've never felt more self-conscious in my life. Carefully, I walk down the stage and turn around, making sure I don't misstep. I'm not usually clumsy, but right now, anything could happen. It feels like I'm detached from my body.

Once I've finished the walk, I step down into the holding area. It is heavily lit, but at this level, I can survey the men watching. I sit down and glance up at the crowd. Most of the men are old enough to be my grandfather, which makes this sickening.

My gaze halts on a pair of emerald eyes staring right back at me. It feels like my heart skips a beat as I let myself admire the handsome man's appearance. He's got short brown hair and a neatly trimmed beard. Tattoos run up his neck and exposed arms.

When I return my attention to his face, he's smirking at me with an almost manic look. It sends shivers racing down my spine. That man is certainly attractive, but I can tell from the look in his eyes he's not the kind of man you ever want to meet.

I look away from him, feeling the heat traveling around my body at the way he looks at me. Maybe it's best that one of the old guys buy me, as it will probably be over quicker that way.

It's only one night.

I repeat the same phrase repeatedly in my mind, trying to justify this crazy thing I'm doing. My mother would kill me for being so foolish. She'll never learn the truth about how I found the cash for her procedures.

The girl who had stood next to me leans toward me as we sit in the holding area. "Is it just me, or does it feel like we're pieces of meat at a meat market?"

I meet her gaze and shake my head. "It's not just you. I won't deny this is fucked up, to be honest."

She laughs, but it's laced with anxiety. "Yeah, I'm wondering if I made a mistake. It's all shady, but I need the money."

I sigh heavily. "Me too."

They invite the rest of the girls onto the stage who pack into the holding area. The girl, whose name I don't know, tries to engage in small talk. I'm not exactly in the mood for talking. My insides are churning, and I'm focusing on not throwing up.

My attention returns to the audience. I find my eyes are drawn to the man I'd seen staring at me before. My heart skips a beat when I see he's still watching me with an intense gaze that sets my face ablaze. I hold his gaze for a few beats, and he still won't look away. It's clear that I've caught his interest.

I clear my throat and look anywhere else. The look in that man's eyes makes me believe that the last thing I want is for him to bid on me. It's one that is dark and twisted. He may be attractive, but I think I'd take any of the older men over him in this club.

"Did you know that the auction prices often exceed

a million dollars?" The girl who spoke to me earlier asks.

My brow furrows. "Where did you hear that?"

"My friend did this before me. She got just under a million after the fees." She shrugs. "I reckon it's a small price to pay for that kind of money. Not all the girls fetch that much, just the hottest ones."

My stomach churns as I wonder why a man would pay over a million dollars for a night with a virgin. All I hope is that I've not misunderstood the terms of selling my virginity.

"That's insane. Why would a guy pay that much money for a fuck?"

The girl opens her mouth but shuts it as Aleks stands in front of us. "No chitchat, ladies. The auction is starting, so shut up and look pretty."

I clench my jaw at his demeaning attitude and gaze at the stage where the head guy is standing. I'm six women from last in this auction. It seems the girl sitting next to me was right. There's already been about seven bids over a million dollars.

I wonder how many of the women here are selling their virginity to make them rich quickly. It wouldn't surprise me. All I care about is getting enough cash to make my mom better. She sacrificed so much to ensure I went to the best dance school possible, working two jobs. I need to pay it back. I can't lose the only person who means anything to me in this world.

If I were to get over a million dollars in this auction,

I could pay her back for all her hard work. I could buy us an apartment, rather than living in the dive of a place that we rent for too much money.

The likelihood of me fetching that kind of money is slim, but none of the girls tonight have gone for less than five hundred thousand dollars. It will change our lives completely, even after all the fees are taken.

"Now, we're onto number twenty-two. Let's start the bidding at two hundred thousand."

My stomach churns as I realize how close it is to my time. I have been purposely avoiding looking toward the brutally handsome man at the front. The one that seems to have taken a shine to me. I glance over in his direction, and he is still staring at me.

He smiles at me, but it's not exactly a kind smile.

I lick my bottom lip and wonder what it would be like to be in bed with him. A gut-wrenching sensation pulls at my stomach at the thought of him touching me. There's no doubt he's attractive; at first glance, he's one of the more attractive men in the club.

Although I'm here and selling my virginity, I haven't given the act much thought. I knew if I thought about it too much, I'd chicken out before I got here. My intimacy issues stem from childhood and my father, who I haven't seen since I was eight years old.

He used to abuse me whenever my mother was at work, making me touch him inappropriately. One night, they sent her home sick and walked in on it happening.

I was forever thankful that she called the cops and got him arrested.

It never went beyond touching, but something tells me it would have gotten worse if it wasn't for her catching him when she did. I never knew how to tell her as a little kid. My father told me she wouldn't believe me if I did.

From that moment on, it's been just my mom and me. We have an incredibly close bond, and she worked hard to pay for my therapy from an early age. Therapy has helped me mend a lot of the damage he did, but it's still difficult for me to trust people, especially men. Even though my mom stole me away from the abuse, I felt it robbed me of my childhood—my innocence.

In high school, boys would ask me out, but my fear of intimacy always stopped me from accepting. In some ways, I think selling my virginity takes away the emotional aspect of it. I don't know if I'm making a huge mistake. All I know is that I will do anything to save my mom's life.

It may not be a brilliant move auctioning off my virginity with my past. I have no other avenue to turn to. We could end up on the streets if I can't get enough money to pay rent and make the debt repayments.

The bidding on number Twenty-two ends, and I can feel my nerves spiking out of control. When I glance back at the man who had been staring, all his attention is now on the auctioneer.

"Next up is number twenty-three." The auctioneer

clears his throat, and I hold my breath, waiting for him to start the bidding. "Let's start the bid for this beauty at five hundred thousand."

My heart skips a beat. That's the highest starting price tonight. I feel my cheeks heat that the auctioneer singled me out to start so high. I watch the handsome man who had been watching me so intently.

He is watching as the bidding moves swiftly past the million-dollar mark. My jaw is on the floor as the men keep bidding, pushing it toward a million and a half dollars. There's no doubt that we are going to be set for a long while with this kind of cash, but I can't help the niggling doubt in my mind that I haven't thought this through. No man would pay this kind of money for one fuck.

"Can I get one million five hundred and fifty? Anyone?"

I watch, waiting to see if anyone bids. The handsome man who had been watching me lifts his paddle and enters the competition.

I can't understand why I want him to win me. Perhaps it's because of the chemistry between us. Being attracted to the man that buys my virginity would surely make this entire ordeal easier. The only other guy in the race now is old enough to be my grandfather.

It feels as though time slows down as all my attention remains fixed on the handsome man. He's calm and collected as he continues to bid higher. I no longer listen to the numbers as the auctioneer keeps pushing the bids. All the while, I watch him, hoping that if I'm lucky, he will be the last in the race.

When I looked into his eyes, I could see the darkness that I recognize too well. A darkness that I have growing and twisting inside of me too. That's the only thing that scares me.

Would I be better off with the old man?

The man I want to win me bids two million dollars, and my eyes widen. I stare at him in shock, not expecting him to glance my way. When he does, I feel my cheeks heat. I can't bring myself to break the eye contact as it sends shock waves through my core.

I get a feeling that he won't back off. He's confident he's going to win. I guess I'll soon have the answer to my question when he finally takes me home.

Will the darkness inside of this man be too much for me to handle?

4

MALACHY

*S*he's an angel sent from heaven.

I don't normally find myself so enamored with any of the women I buy at this auction, but number twenty-three has caught my eye in ways I can't quite explain.

Her long, fiery red hair frames her beautiful pale complexion. The moment she stepped onto that stage, I knew I had to have her. I hadn't even looked at her perfectly curvy body. Her unmatchable beauty captured all my attention.

All of her physical attributes pale compared to her piercing blue eyes. Eyes that hold emotion that I know all too well—self-loathing. It felt like I was looking into a mirror as she stared back at me.

The auctions are going high tonight. I think number twenty-three is going to be the most expensive if the murmurs that broke out across the room when she stepped onto the stage are anything to go by. She's worth it, though. I know most of the men here don't have the level of disposable cash that I have, except perhaps Mikhail.

I won't let her slip through my fingers. She has noticed me more than once, staring at her, but I can't help it. That woman is perfect. A part of me considers how I'm going to approach this. Normally my goal is to break the virgins that think I pay the money I do all so I can fuck them once. Breaking this angel doesn't seem so appealing.

I crack my neck as tension builds at the unusual thoughts I'm having about this virgin. It's a warning sign. A sign that I shouldn't bid on her. Yet a deep, dark, primal side of me knows I can't let another man touch her. She's mine already.

Her number is the next up. I can see men readying themselves around me with their paddles. It sends adrenaline spiking through my veins. No one will take her from me. I'll pay as much as necessary to get what I want.

"Next up is number twenty-three." The auctioneer clears his throat. "Let's start the bid for this beauty at five hundred thousand."

The bastard knows she's going to be popular, starting it so high. I don't show my hand yet as a guy at the table next to me holds up his paddle. There's no point bidding at the start.

"Thank you. Can I get six hundred?"

A guy in the back increases the bid, and it climbs to one million dollars in record speed. The guy next to me bows out, but two others are battling it out for her in the back. I turn my attention to the angel whose eyes are wide as she watches the men bid hideous amounts of money to take her innocence. She has seen nothing yet.

The bidding gets to one and a half million, and one guy stops. It's my time to strike.

"Can I get one million five hundred and fifty? Anyone?"

I hold my paddle up in response.

"Thank you, sir," he says.

"One million six hundred and fifty?" he asks.

The guy bids instantly, and it's clear that he's in it for the long-haul. I was surveying him during the bidding. Whoever he is, he's not a regular here.

I hold my paddle up. "Two million," I call, loud enough for everyone to hear me. As I do, I glance over at number twenty-three.

Her eyes are wide as she stares back.

"Okay, upping the stakes. Anyone for two and a quarter million?"

The guy at the back hesitates before raising his paddle. He's close to his limit.

"Thank you, sir," the auctioneer says, glancing in my direction. "Two and a half?" I nod and wave my paddle.

"Sir, two and three quarters?"

He glares in my direction before stiffly shaking his head.

"Okay, going once, going twice, sold for two and a half million dollars to Mr. McCarthy." He glances down into the holding area. "You know the procedure."

I nod and knock back the rest of my whiskey as they lead my purchase away to get ready to leave with me. My stomach twists with what I can only describe as nerves at the anticipation of meeting my virgin. It's weird and a little unnerving.

Number twenty-three differs from my previous purchases. For a start, she's the single most beautiful woman I've ever seen in my life. The clawing desire to go back there before she's dressed in her clothes is tempting, but I know it's against the rules.

Buyers must collect their purchases and take them away from the club before acting on any sick and twisted desires we might have.

"That was an expensive purchase," Jameson says.

I tilt my head and glare at him. "I see you haven't bid on anyone as usual."

He shakes his head. "No one took my fancy."

"Bullshit," I reply, slamming my whiskey glass down on the table and standing. "You don't have the money to buy any of these girls. You're like the rest of the dirty perverts that come to stare at something you can't afford to buy."

A muscle in his jaw ticks. But he knows I'm right. Jameson has been coming to these events longer than I have and never once bought a girl, merely bidding at the start and dropping out early. The guy is pathetic.

Without saying goodbye, I turn my back on him and make my way toward the back room of the club. They won't let me in if she's not ready, but I couldn't stand sitting with that politician for any longer than necessary.

I knock on the door of the changing room, and Aleks answers. "She's almost ready. I'll bring her to you." He shows me a piece of paper. "Will you make the transfer from the usual account?"

I nod. "I've already asked my man to transfer the amount owed. He's confirmed it's done."

"Good. You must have really wanted the bitch to pay so much money for her."

I clench my jaw, feeling irritated by this Russian calling her a bitch. It makes no sense why that would annoy me since I haven't even met her.

"Send her out to me as soon as she is ready." I turn my back on Aleks and wait to one side. The door slams shut.

Something is intriguing to me about my redhead virgin. I'm impatient to meet her and learn her name. It's not often that I'm impatient for anything.

The door behind me swings open, and this time it's not Aleks standing there. My redhead virgin stands in the doorway. Her captivating blue eyes are filled with uncertainty.

Aleks stands behind her. "Follow your master, bitch."

My jaw clenches, as I hate hearing him call her that again. I hold out my outstretched hand to her, and she stares at it hesitantly. "Take my hand."

Her eyes move from my hand and back to my face. When our eyes meet, I feel a shock of need pulsing through me.

I clear my throat. "I said, take my hand. Are you deaf?"

She shakes her head and slowly takes my hand. The tension in her grip is apparent, as is the same with all the women I bid on. The difference is I pay more attention to this girl. I tighten my grip on her hand and drag her toward the exit of the club.

She trips over her feet as I pull her out of the door toward my car. I steady her, wrapping an arm around her before she can lose her footing.

"Don't trip over, lass," I say, feeling my breath escape me as her striking blue eyes find mine.

She laughs nervously. "I'm always such a klutz." My virgin breaks the lingering eye contact, brushing a hair out of her face and looking anywhere but at me.

"Come on," I say, keeping my hand on her hip and pulling her toward the Chevy. When I stop and unlock the car, her eyes widen.

"Wow, nice car. A 1967 Impala?" She asks.

I can't help but smile that she likes my car, even better that she knew the year. "Sure is. You a fan of classic cars then, lass?"

She hugs her arms around her waist and nods.

"Yeah, I love old cars. They don't make them like this anymore."

Admiration for this girl I don't even know pulses through me. She's more stunning than an angel, and she likes old classic American cars–a passion of mine. "True, you can't beat a classic." I wink at her, making her cheeks stain a deep pink.

I open the door to the driver's side, and she opens hers. A tense silence falls between us as we sit in the car together. The girl clasps her fingers in her lap and fidgets with them nervously.

I force my attention away from her and turn over the engine, feeling the purr of it melt away my concerns over the odd connection with this virgin.

There's a doubt tugging at my insides as I drive out of the club, heading south toward my home.

I never doubt myself. Out of all the virgins I've bought and fucked, none of them made me doubt what I was doing. Sex for me is a release and nothing more. I don't enjoy fucking whores as they bore me, but I've yet to find a woman with any integrity that's into my tastes.

The virgin auction gives me the perfect supply of untouched women to break and bend to my will. My dark and twisted tastes are often too much for most of the virgins I buy, although some learned to love it before I tired of them.

I know many assholes think my constant presence at those auctions is immoral, but morals don't apply to me.

I'm the leader of a powerful mafia organization. I don't have time for morals.

I swallow hard as everything about the redhead beauty sitting beside me is made to entice. She smells of pure fucking sin. The scent of lavender coming from her seems to fill the car and flood my senses. My cock has been hard ever since I took her hand back at the club. It's making it difficult to think straight.

I shift myself in my pants, trying to ease the pressure. When I buy a virgin, I never touch them the first night as I like to make them sweat. My unexplainable desire for her is going to make keeping my hands off her difficult.

I focus all my attention on the road and try to keep my urges in check. The last thing I need is to lose control. Control is my anchor, and if I lose it, I could lose everything.

5

SCARLETT

I'm still in a state of shock as I sit in the passenger's seat of my purchaser's Chevy. The organizers have wired me an eighty percent share of two and a half million dollars, all for this guy sitting next to me to fuck me.

There must be a catch. All I know is that whatever it is, it will be worth it to have my mom set for the rest of her life. We'll be able to get her the best cancer treatment and buy a place outright.

All for one night. It seems too good to be true.

"So, lass. Have you got a name?"

I glance over at the rough-looking man who paid a hideous amount of money to take me home tonight. "Yes, Scarlett."

He smiles as he keeps his eyes on the road. "Scarlett," he says my name slowly, and it sounds dirty coming from his lips. "I like it. My name is Malachy."

He has a distinct Irish accent which only adds to his allure.

I clear my throat. "It's good to meet you."

He laughs, and it sends shivers down my spine. "Not sure that's what you will say once you get to know me."

My stomach sinks. "Get to know you?"

He glances at me briefly, smirking manically. "Don't tell me you thought I paid two and a half million dollars for one night, darlin'?"

The way he says darling makes my stomach churn. His accent makes it sound sexy, but it's also too intimate a word from a man I don't know. I tense and inch myself away from him a little, feeling my walls erect.

Taking a deep breath, I try to remember my therapy. I should have known that it was too good to be true. Malachy has no intention of letting me go after one night. "I thought I sold you my virginity, so once you take it, then I'm free?" I ask, knowing how naïve I must sound.

He clicks his tongue and shakes his head. "Who said I'm going to take it right away?"

I swallow hard. "I can't be away from home for too long. My mom is sick."

That gets his attention as he stares at me with those piercing emerald eyes. "Is that why you auctioned your virginity?"

I nod in response. "It was the only way to pay her hospital bills."

Malachy shakes his head. "Well, you won't be able

to return to your usual life for a month or two on average." His brow furrows, as if he can't believe what he is saying. "I can get someone to make sure she is comfortable, though, using the money you got from the auction."

I know I can't abandon my mother in her time of need. She's always been there for me. Although we needed the money, I'm not sure how she will cope without me. "Surely, I can see her, even if I'm staying with you?"

"No, darlin'. You're mine now, and that means you do as I say. You will remain in my home, and there's no room for negotiation."

Panic claws at my throat. "What if I refuse?"

He laughs that sharp, villainous laugh that sends tremors of dread through me. "If you refuse, then you can give me my two and a half million dollars back."

My stomach sinks as I stare out of the window, realizing that I've landed myself in the hands of a monster. The fact is my mom needs the money to treat her cancer more than she needs me by her side. I have no idea how I'm going to explain my disappearing act to her.

My head pounds as the pressure and reality of what I've done weighs heavily on me. Greg will never hold my waitressing job for me. It means once I get out of this man's grasp, I'll be jobless. I don't ask him if I'll be able to keep my job, as I know the answer.

An uneasy silence falls between us for the rest of the

drive. He pulls up to an enormous set of gates that open electronically. The mansion hidden behind the gates and up a driveway is enormous. I expected as much since he had a spare two and a half million dollars to bid on me.

There are four men inside the gates, all with machine guns. I feel my stomach twist and glance at the man in the driver's seat. Whoever this man is, he's dangerous. I knew that the moment I looked into his eyes, but perhaps I underestimated how dangerous.

Malachy glances at me and shrugs. "I'm an important and rich man. Security is a necessity."

I say nothing, knowing that even rich men don't have security with machine guns. Pistols, maybe, but not machine guns. He parks in front of the mansion and turns off the engine, still holding the steering wheel.

"Come on," he says, opening the door and getting out of the car.

I open the car door and get out, staring up at the mansion towering ahead of me. It's daunting and about one-thousand times bigger than our little apartment in central Boston.

Suddenly, Malachy appears to the right of me and places an arm around my back, sending shivers down my spine. "I'll give you the grand tour."

He keeps his arm against my back as he leads me firmly toward the front door. My nerves are firing out of control as he half drags me up the grand stone steps into my inescapable fate. I can't say that I'm regretting my actions yet, even if this lasts a month. My eighty percent share of the money is life-changing for my mom and me.

I'm a bag of nerves as he opens the front door to an opulent hallway decked in travertine marble that glimmers as the light reflects off the surface. An enormous crystal chandelier hangs in the center of the circular entrance hall in front of a double staircase, which leads up to the second floor. The place is beyond luxurious and by far the most beautiful home I've ever stepped foot in.

I'm so in awe of the sight in front of me. I almost forgot Malachy's firm touch—a touch that is too intimate. Until he squeezes my hip, making me tense.

"You must be tired. I'll show you to my room."

I swallow hard at the mention of his room. He said he doesn't intend to take what he paid so handsomely for tonight. So why am I staying in his room?

A sense of dread sinks my stomach as I wonder what I've gotten myself into. Malachy lets go of my hip and takes my hand instead, leading me up the right-hand side of the staircase. Once we get to the top, he turns right down a corridor toward a door at the end.

My heart pounds frantically in my ears as I walk by this man's side. I feel like a lamb being led to the slaughter. What lies behind that door is entirely unknown.

I swallow hard as Malachy lets go of my hand, opening the door. "After you, darlin'," he purrs, making my stomach flutter.

I force myself to step inside and glance around the room. It's huge like the rest of his home is, and there's a giant four-poster bed against the back wall, pride of place in the center. My stomach twists when I notice shackles affixed to each post.

I bite my tongue and try to ignore the warning bells going off in my head. This guy is into BDSM, and I don't know what to think of that. My inexperience makes the entire situation overwhelming.

"Get freshened up and pick out a dress in the closet." He nods to a door to the right of the bed. "Come downstairs in an hour, and we'll have a late dinner together." His emerald green eyes pin me to the spot as he stares at me with an intensity that makes my blood boil. There is no question in his voice. These are orders.

I nod in response, but Malachy moves closer. I feel the walls closing in on me as he grabs my hips hard and tugs me against him.

"Whenever I ask you to do something, I want you to reply with yes, sir," he orders.

My stomach twists as I stare up at the rough man holding me. Swallowing hard, I nod and say what he wants to hear. "Yes, sir."

He smirks at me. "Good girl. Now, get ready. I'll see you in an hour." He winks before turning and walking out of the room.

I watch the way his every step is filled with such easy confidence. He doesn't look back at me as he shuts the door behind him.

Sighing, I glance around the room. My mom will be worried about me if I don't let her know I'm not coming home tonight. The question is how I'm going to explain not coming home for the next month or two.

I pull my cell phone from my pocket and type out a text to her.

Hope you are feeling okay. I will not be back tonight. Staying at Kaia's. Let me know if you need anything. Love you.

My stomach twists as I hit send. Whatever my mom might need, I can't be there for her. This man has bailed us out, but he won't allow me to see her. It's cruel, considering he knows she's ill.

I walk toward the bed and sit on it. The mattress is ridiculously comfortable, and the comforter is pure silk. I can hardly believe how soft it is to the touch. I reach for the draw in the nightstand and open it, curious about the man I'm going to lose my virginity to.

My stomach twists when I see it is home to a couple of whips, an enormous bottle of lube, blindfolds, and a variety of dildos and plugs. This man isn't into vanilla sex. He's into alternate, kinky shit that I'm not sure I can be down with. Something tells me it doesn't matter if I can handle it or not. He will get his way or have his money back. The latter I can't afford.

I shut the drawer and open the next one. The contents of it makes my stomach sink. There are a few knives and a gun. I shut the drawer and jump away from it, standing and glancing around the room.

What kind of man have I allowed to bring me home?

When I look into his eyes, I see a dark and tortured soul. From the contents of this drawer, I wonder if I'm underestimating the darkness that lies within. Malachy already alluded that it won't be good to meet him once I get to know him. The danger that lies in my future here scares me more than I'd like to admit. My mom always taught me to face my fears with my head held high.

I feel that selling my virginity out of desperation to get us out of debt and facing my intimacy issues isn't what she had in mind. The more I think about it, the more I believe I've made a grave mistake.

There's no pulling out now. Malachy owns me until he says so.

6

MALACHY

*I*t's been longer than an hour as I stand in the hallway, tapping my feet on the travertine. Scarlett will have to learn that punctuality is key for me. I won't tolerate tardiness or disobedience.

I'm about to rush up the stairs and give her a piece of my mind when she appears. My rage eases the moment I see her standing there in the most exquisite gold dress with a plunging neckline that shows off the soft curves of her large breasts.

My cock hardens, and my rage turns to pure lust. I lick my bottom lip at the thought of ravishing my virgin. Hunger for food isn't what I feel right now. I'd rather feast on my expensive little virgin.

Her cheeks are stained pink when my attention returns to her face. Slowly, she walks down the steps toward me. Each of her steps hesitant and for a good reason.

She's walking toward a man so dark she could never comprehend the tortured soul within me. I'm bent and broken, and it's the reason I take so much pleasure in bending and breaking others.

"You look like a dream, darlin'," I say, reaching for her hand and pulling her close.

She tenses the moment I touch her, making me wonder why she's so uptight. There's something different about Scarlett that I can't put my finger on.

"You must be hungry," I purr into her ear, gently biting her earlobe.

The gesture makes her tense more. Scarlett is like a statue in my arms, barely even breathing as I hold her close.

I pull back and look into her striking blue eyes. They're filled with what I could only describe as pure terror. A terror that cuts me to my core in ways I can't explain.

Clearing my throat, I step back from her. "Follow me." I don't mention her reluctance to be intimate with me. Normally the virgins I buy aren't so repulsed by me this early on.

I lead her toward the dining room. Her heels click on the travertine floor, signaling that she's following me. The table is set with dishes of food and our place settings opposite each other across the table.

I hold out Scarlett's seat and glance at her. "You'll sit here."

She takes her seat, sweeping the hair from her face.

I take my seat on the opposite side of the table and meet her anxious gaze. "Tuck in, darlin'."

She swallows hard and glances at the food in front of her. "There's a lot of choice."

I guess there is, but I've gotten used to it. Gone are the days I used to beg for scraps on the street, hoping I could scrounge enough food so Alicia wouldn't go hungry. I've known true hunger. What it's like to feel so hungry you wonder if you're going to carry on. I think it's the reason I always insist my staff make me such a varied spread.

Although, I've never forgotten where I've come from. The food never goes to waste. "I like variety," I respond.

She nods and grabs a bread roll and some butter.

I raise a brow at her bland choice. "All this choice, and you go for bread and butter?"

Scarlett shrugs. "I'm not hungry, and my stomach is churning."

I bite the inside of my cheek, knowing I'm the reason for her unease. The virgins are always uneasy around me, so I can't understand why I care that I'm making her nervous. "Don't be anxious, lass."

She looks up at me, as if surprised by my feeble attempt to calm her. "It's kind of hard not to be given the circumstances."

I crack my neck, wondering why I'm even bothering to calm her down. The girls are always more fun when they're on edge. It means I can toy with them easily. "True," I reply, digging into the food in front of me.

I don't apologize for the way I eat. Although she looks at me like I'm mad. You can take the lad out of the street, but you can't take the street out of the lad. At least, that's my excuse. I love eating with my hands and have done since I was twelve years old.

Who needs cutlery?

I didn't need it on the streets, and I don't need it now. "What are you staring at, darlin'?"

She flushes every single time I call her that. It makes me want to do it more. "Nothing." She shakes her head.

I laugh at her bashfulness. It's cute, but it will soon disappear once I've had her writhing beneath me later tonight. Her virginity will remain intact, but I won't spend the night by her side without tasting her. Scarlett is the most expensive virgin I've bought, and something tells me I won't tire of her so quickly.

"You won't be so embarrassed around me later tonight, lass."

Her eyes widen, and she searches my face questioningly. "I thought you said you wouldn't—"

"Take your virginity tonight? No, but there are other ways for me to explore your perfect body'."

Her flush cheeks pale, and it looks like she's about to throw up. "Oh no," she mutters as she looks down at her plate.

"You're not going to be sick, are you?" I ask.

She shakes her head. "No." There's a sudden harshness to her tone. "I'm fine."

I find Scarlett intriguing—like a puzzle I want to solve. I finish eating my chicken wings and ribs, licking my fingers clean once finished. Scarlett only picked at some salad and ate the bread roll, which is a real waste of some good meat. Not that it will go to waste. Anything that my family or I don't eat that could go bad is anonymously donated to the local soup kitchens for the homeless.

"Are you finished?" I ask, tilting my head to the side slightly.

She reluctantly looks at me, making eye contact. Every time our eyes meet, it feels like an electric shock pulses through my veins. "Yes." The column of her throat bobs as she holds my gaze. "What now?"

I smirk at her. "Not sure you want the answer to that question, darlin'." I shrug. "But it's time to get you into my bed." My cock pulses in my pants at the mere thought of lying next to this beauty.

She swallows hard. "Can I ask you one question?"

I narrow my eyes at her. Normally, I'd say no. Since I want to learn more about Scarlett, I decide to indulge her. "One question."

She exhales deeply. "What do you do for a living?"

I shouldn't answer truthfully, but I don't hide who I am from people. The cops I have on my side would protect me if I needed it. "I lead the Irish mafia in Boston."

Her eyes practically bulge out of her head. Scarlett turns paler. "Mafia?"

I nod in response. "The details aren't important. All you need to know is I'm a dangerous man." I hold her gaze. "So don't think about fucking with me. Do you understand?" I fear my treatment of her this far has been too soft. Scarlett can't get the wrong idea about what this is. A business arrangement that I have handsomely paid her for.

"Yes, sir," Scarlett answers quietly, glancing down at her plate.

I clap my hands, which makes her jump. "Good, now follow me." I stand and walk toward the exit of the dining room, stopping at the door when I don't hear her follow. "What are you waiting for, lass?"

Scarlett doesn't move, frozen in her seat.

I growl in frustration and walk back to her chair. Her eyes are misted with tears as she stares at her entwined hands in her lap. "I said, follow me." I grab her arm and yank her to her feet.

She places a hand on my chest to steady herself. Her touch lights me on fire as she stares into my eyes. The fear is present whenever I get close. I clench my jaw, wishing I didn't have this odd sensation to calm her fears. Gently, I wrap a hand around her throat and bring my face an inch from hers. "I told you not to fuck with me, darlin'. Don't make me regret buying you." With that, I let go of her throat and grab her hand instead.

48

I don't say another word as I lead her up the stairs. Her grip on my hand is slack, but I hold firm. It's best to set out expectations from the start. Scarlett is my plaything that I paid a lot of money for. She needs to learn about her place fast.

I open the door to my room. "Inside," I order.

Her lip quivers as she takes a step inside. Scarlett stands awkwardly in the center, waiting for another order. "Strip and lie on the bed."

Her eyes widen. I wonder if she's going to refuse as a few moments tick by. Finally, she reaches for the strap of her golden dress and eases it off her shoulder. It's a sensual move, even though she doesn't intend it to be. The slowness in her movements is born out of a resistance to do as I say.

My cock throbs in the confines of my pants at the sight of her creamy skin and luscious curves. Scarlett holds her hands in front of her nervously, attempting to cover up. She looks anywhere but at me.

"I want it all off," I order, resisting the urge to walk over to her and tear her lingerie from her perfect, tight body.

Scarlett meets my gaze, and this time there's anger burning in her dazzling blue eyes. It looks like my timid little virgin might have more bite than I bargained for. "Why are you making me strip? You told me you wouldn't take my virginity tonight."

I grind my teeth together, trying to contain my irritation. In two strides, I'm next to her. Slowly, I wrap my fingers around the slender column of her neck.

Scarlett shudders, meeting my gaze with a heat that almost burns my soul. No matter how much she tries to fight, she has wanted me since our eyes met in that club.

"Let us get something straight before we start." I draw in a deep breath, inhaling her sweet scent. "I paid two and a half million dollars for you. I own you. I control you. You are mine to do with as I want until I say so. Do you understand?"

Her throat bobs beneath my hands. "Yes," she says, but there's irritation in her voice.

I press my lips to the edge of her jaw, teasing the tips of my teeth over her skin. "Yes, master," I order.

She glares at me with a ferocity that tells me she's going to be one of the harder ones. "Yes, master," she says sarcastically.

I tighten my grip on her throat. "You won't use that tone with me, Scarlett. Do you understand?"

Fear ignites in her striking blue eyes as she stares at me for a few beats, struggling to draw breath into her lungs. Scarlett nods her head frantically, giving me the signal to loosen my grasp.

She grasps her throat and stares at me with wide eyes. "You almost choked me to death."

I shake my head. "Don't be so dramatic, lass." I let my eyes dip to her figure. "Now, lingerie off, and don't make me ask again."

She nods, hooking her finger into the waistband of

her panties first. There's a moment of hesitation as she glares at me before exhaling shakily and dropping them to the floor.

My already rock-hard cock leaks into my tight boxer briefs. I'm ready to sink every inch deep into my pretty little virgin, but it's too soon. The desire I have for this girl outweighs anything I've felt before.

She nervously unhooks her bra, seemingly uncertain about stripping in front of me. It's strange as I've seen her naked before at the auction. Perhaps it's because we're alone now, and she feels vulnerable. I can't understand why the normal desire to scare and terrorize isn't there. All I want to do is protect her instead.

"Don't worry, darlin'. I won't hurt you."

She meets my gaze and raises a brow. "I don't know if I can believe that." She pulls the bra off and drops it to the floor, instinctively crossing her arms over her chest.

I growl softly and move toward her. "Don't cover yourself."

The fear in her eyes differs from other girls I've had in this position. I pry her arms from her chest gently and groan at the sight of her perfect, round breasts and hard, peaked nipples. Gently, I move my mouth to cover one and suck.

Scarlett gasps softly, reaching for my shoulders as her knees shake. Her touch only fuels my insatiable lust for this woman. I move to her other nipple and lavish the same attention on it. This time she moans softly, her eyes rolling back as she enjoys the attention.

"I'll only make you feel good, lass," I say, kissing a path up her neck, surprising myself with the gentleness I'm handling her with. "Now be a good girl and lie down on the bed."

She meets my gaze with dilated eyes. There's still hesitation there, but she does as I say.

I watch as she lies on the bed with her legs tightly pressed together and her hands over her chest. It seems my order has gone unheeded.

"Legs open and hands by your side before I tie them up so you can't cover up your perfect tits."

Scarlett licks her lips before placing her hands by her side, clenching them into fists.

Slowly, she opens her legs so I can get a perfect view of her tight little cunt. I rub a hand across my straining cock in my pants. Part of me wants to bury myself deep inside of her.

I walk toward her, grabbing hold of her thighs and parting them wider. "So fucking beautiful," I murmur, mesmerized by her. I grab hold of the chains fixed to my bed, clamping them around her ankles.

Scarlett tenses the moment she is restrained, staring at me with that same petrified look. A creeping sense of doubt enters my mind.

What has this girl been through?

Why do I even care?

I shake my head, trying to rid myself of the stupid

thoughts pulsing through my mind. I grab her wrists next and fix them in chains too. There's something about this girl that gets to me. Maybe I shouldn't have bid on her. Maybe I should have bought one of the boring girls on the stage.

"What are you going to do?" she asks, her voice so small and fragile. A contrast to the relatively confident girl I've witnessed up to now.

I groan as my cock pulses against the fabric of my briefs. "Taste you, darlin'."

Her eyes widen, and she stiffens more.

"Relax and enjoy it. I'm going to make you feel better than you've felt before."

Her thighs shudder beneath my hands. I unbuckle my pants, needing to be freed from the confining fabric.

Scarlett sits up slightly, watching me like a hawk. The concern on her face melts to intrigue as she stares at the hard outline of my cock. It's impossible not to groan at the way her eyes dilate. "Do you want to see me too, darlin'?"

Scarlett bites her lip, looking unsure. Finally, she nods her head.

Fuck.

I've never wanted a girl the way I want her. Keeping my cock out of her perfect virgin pussy is going to be harder than I expected. I pull off my boxer briefs, watching as her eyes widen and she swallows hard.

The sight of her throat bobbing like that brings a new dirty fucking image to my mind. I want her to swallow every inch of my cock down that pretty little throat. "Fuck, I want you so bad, lass." I fist the base of my cock up and down, overcome by my desire. "Now, lie back and let me taste you."

She docsn't hesitate this time, resting her head on the pillow.

I continue to fist my cock in my hand and lower my mouth between her thighs. Softly, I lick between her soaking wet lips.

I groan. "You taste like heaven, baby," I murmur before sucking on her clit.

Scarlett's hips buck, and she moans so loud. The sound knocks the air from my lungs as I start to devour her. I'm desperate to hear her moan repeatedly.

Pain is always my starting point. I can't understand why I've gone straight to pleasure with Scarlett. A desire to make her want me rules me. It's a desire I've never come across before.

I want Scarlett to want me as badly as I want her. Slowly, I slide a finger into her tight, wet pussy.

She gasps, staring down at me as I fuck her with my finger. "Please, don't—" I find the spot inside of her that lights her up, stopping her mid-sentence. "Fuck," she cries out, shutting her eyes.

"Don't what, baby?" I watch her face as I continue to finger fuck her. "Don't make you come all over my fingers?"

She bites her lip as her entire face flushes a deeper pink. "I-I don't—"

I suck her clit again, and that's all it takes. My pretty little virgin comes all over my finger and tongue, driving me wild. I lap up every drop, desperate to devour her.

Once I've finished, I rotate the shackles on the bed and grab her hips. "On your hands and knees."

A visible shiver pulses through her body as she moves to her hands and knees. The sight is beyond satisfying. I press my finger against her tight little asshole.

Scarlett tenses. "What are you—"

I lightly spank her ass, so softly it would barely hurt. "No questions." I groan as my cock leaks onto the bedsheets. I fist myself in my hand and focus my attention on her tight asshole.

I probe my tongue against the tight ring of muscles. Scarlett tenses beneath me as I lick her in such an intimate place. Her pussy practically gushes over the bedsheets.

My cock spills onto the bedsheets, too, as I crave release. The thought of my seed dripping between her ass cheeks drives me insane. I never lose control like this, but Scarlett has a way of bringing the possessive side of me to the surface.

"Moan for me, baby," I order, continuing to devour her ass.

She groans instead, writhing to get out of my grip. "Please, stop—"

I growl and spank her ass with my hand. "Don't pretend it doesn't feel good, darlin'. You are dripping everywhere." I run a finger through her pussy. I release her wrists and ankles from the restraints. "Lie on your back," I order.

She does as I say, flipping onto her back and staring up at me with innocent, wide eyes. Scarlett may be a virgin, but she's not innocent. There's a darkness inside of her—darkness that I recognize all too well.

"I want you to play with yourself until you come." I hold her gaze as it widens slightly. "Then, I'm going to cover that pretty little cunt of yours in my cum."

Scarlett gasps at my use of that word.

"Do you understand, lass?"

She nods, forgetting my instruction. I grab her throat softly. "How did I tell you to respond to my questions?"

"Yes, master," she says, her voice laced with unmistakable desire.

I can't understand why her using that term doesn't satisfy me as much as it should. There's something off about it I can't quite place.

I grab the shaft of my cock as Scarlett slips her hands between her thighs.

We both fixate on each other. She keeps her gaze on my throbbing, hard cock as she plunges her fingers in and out of her wet pussy. It's an amazing sight, watching my horny little virgin turn into a desperate little whore in front of my eyes. "That's it, darlin', fuck your pussy for me," I growl, fisting my cock harder and faster.

She moans, lips parting in a way that makes me

want to kiss them. I refrain, as it's too intimate. "Oh god," she says, as she slides her fingers to her clit and rubs herself.

"I want you to scream my name as you come undone."

Her bright blue eyes find mine, dilated with such longing. "Yes, master," she says, her voice so innocent and sweet.

I'm struggling to hold on, waiting for her to come before I unleash my seed all over her.

"Fuck." Her hips rise from the bed as she pushes herself toward the edge. "Yes, Malachy," she cries my name as she comes undone, juice gushing from between her thighs.

The sight alone brings my release. I grunt as rope after rope of cum flies out of my cock, coating my little virgin's pussy and stomach.

Scarlett stares down with wide eyes, watching as I come apart. She licks her thick bottom lip, which makes me think dirty fucking thoughts. I drag a finger through my cum and bring it to her mouth. "Taste me, baby," I order.

Her eyes widen, but she doesn't hesitate. Scarlett opens her mouth and allows me to slide it inside. Like an obedient little whore, she sucks it clean, moaning as she does.

I notice her relax against the pillows, shutting her eyes as if we're finished. "Don't get too comfortable. I've only just started with you, darlin'." I tease my hand around her throat softly. "I'm going to make you come so many times until you're so tired you can't keep your eyes open."

Her eyes shoot open wide, and she stares into mine questioningly. My cock pulses to life at the thought, as if making her come will never get boring. We're in for a long night.

7

SCARLETT

The next morning, I wake to find Malachy's side of the bed empty. Relief sweeps through me that he's not here. After the dirty things he did to me last night, I don't think I could face him. I groan as I roll over, holding my wrist against my forehead.

The moment I think about it, a pulse ignites between my thighs. I wanted Malachy to fuck me so badly that I shocked myself. He obliterated all my inhibitions the moment he touched me. He wouldn't let me sleep, bringing me to climax over and over again. I've sold myself to a beast. A beast that has barely even started with me yet.

There's something dangerously broken about him. I fear his past may harbor far darker secrets than I can fathom. It makes my situation here more dangerous. Part of me wishes that the old guy had bought me. I'd probably be home now with my mom.

As if thinking about her summoned a text from her, my phone goes off.

Morning, what time shall I expect you home?

I stare at the screen, feeling a deep sadness ignite in my chest. Surely, I can pop in and see her. A way to reassure her I'm fine and explain I'll be staying away for a while. I'll have to tell her I got a new job which needs me to work away.

The thought of lying to the one person I trust the most in this world almost tears me apart. I know that I can't tell her the truth. She wouldn't just be disappointed in me. She'd feel guilty that our desperate situation led me to do something so reckless.

I swing my legs out of bed and get up, determined to see her today. All my life, I've been honest with my mom. Today I'm going to have to lie. It feels wrong, but there's no other option.

I get up and walk to the adjoining bathroom. The bathroom is bigger than my bedroom at home. It's kind of crazy to see how the other half live first-hand. Malachy is by far the richest person I've ever met, even if his means of getting money aren't legal.

I turn on the shower and wait for the water to warm up, tossing my nightdress on the floor. When Malachy said he ran the Irish mafia, I almost wanted to laugh. The mafia is surely a thing of the past. Deep down, I know that's not true. The details around organized crime are hushed up because the police don't want to appear not to be doing their job correctly.

It's frightening that the crazy violence you see in the movies happens every day in a city I've lived in for most of my life. I shower quickly and get ready, unsure how long Malachy will be away. The last thing I want is to be caught sneaking out of this house by him. I know I've hardly seen what that man is capable of.

The corridor outside of the bedroom is deserted. I'm thankful that there's no one around as I make it to the front door. The door isn't even locked. A part of me worries this is going too well. When I step out of the front door, that's when I remember the guards with machine guns.

I have no plan for getting past them. My only option is to walk straight ahead. "Have you just finished too?" A woman speaks behind me.

I turn to face her and see she's wearing a maid's uniform.

"Yeah, I'm just leaving."

She smiles kindly at me. "Let's walk together." She falls into step by my side. "I haven't seen you before. Are you new?"

I nod in response. "Yeah, I started yesterday," I lie, hoping this girl doesn't realize something isn't right.

"Cool, I'm Sienna. What's your name?"

I freeze for a moment, wondering if the staff may know my real name as Malachy's current prisoner. "Alice," I lie.

She holds out a hand. "It's good to meet you."

I shake her hand and smile, despite the nerves

beating around in my stomach. "Yeah, good to meet you too."

We walk toward the gates in silence, and one guy nods at Sienna. "Morning, Sienna. I didn't know you were on night shifts this week."

She nods at the guard. "Morning Kev, yes, unfortunately."

He opens the gate, and we both walk out of it. I can't believe how easy it was to get through the gates, but I'm not sure it would have been without Sienna there.

"Where are you parked?" Sienna asks.

I shake my head. "I don't have a car. I'm going to get the bus."

Her brow furrows. "The bus timetables here are rubbish. You might be waiting an hour."

I nod. "I know, but I can't afford a car right now."

"Where is it you are heading?"

"I live in central Boston."

She nods. "Me too. I can give you a ride?"

I glance down the street toward the bus station, knowing that waiting for the bus is risky. Malachy could return at any moment and spot me. "That would be amazing, if you don't mind."

She shakes her head. "Of course not." She clicks the button on her keys and unlocks a convertible BMW. "Get in."

Malachy must pay his staff well if she can afford such a nice car. I get into the passenger's side of the car and rest my head back, thankful that my escape went without a hitch.

I STARE up at the unkempt apartment block where we've lived for fifteen years. My stomach is churning at the thought of lying to my mom about leaving town for a job. There's no other option.

If all goes well, we will live in luxury in a couple of months once Malachy releases me.

I let out a long, shaky breath before heading inside. My mom can take my bank card linked to the bank with the insane amount of money. At least then, I know she'll be cared for while I'm away.

The debt with the loan shark has already been cleared. I come to the door of our apartment and stare at the crooked number eight on it. There is no going back now. I'm about to lie to the one woman who has done nothing but care for me my entire life.

Pulling my keys out of my bag, I slide it into the lock and open the door. My mom is sitting in her usual spot on the couch, binge-watching her favorite sitcom. She glances over at the door and smiles when she sees me. I can see the bags around her eyes and the dimness of her bright blue pupils. The cancer is weighing her down.

"Hey, sweetheart." She gets up. "Do you want some pancakes for breakfast?"

I smile at her, although my stomach is uneasy. The thought of eating anything right now makes me nauseous, but I've never turned down my mom's pancakes. "Yes, sounds good."

She goes over to the kitchen and gets out the ingredients, but it's impossible not to notice the way her hands shake as she carries the frying pan.

"Why don't you let me do it, Mom." I reach for the handle. "You rest."

She looks frustrated. "I may be sick, but I'm still your mom. I need to look after you."

I smile at how determined she is, but she needs to take it easy. "Let me handle it today. I'm not a little girl anymore."

She nods and goes to sit down as I whisk up the ingredients. All the while, I'm trying to plan out how to break the news to her. I've got to appear happy about the job, but it's almost impossible to appear happy when I'm spinning a lie.

"I've got some good news, Mom."

She glances over at me. "Oh, what's that then?"

I smile at her, the best smile I can muster. "I got a job dancing."

My mom's eyes widen, and she beams at me. "That's amazing news." She hesitates a moment. "Does it pay well?"

I grind my teeth together. "Very well. I got an advance on my pay, and I've cleared the debt with the loan shark."

My mom's eyes widen. "Really? What kind of job is it?"

I feel a sinking dread twisting my stomach as the words leave my mouth. "It's a Broadway production. I'm going to have to be away for a month or two in New York."

Mom claps her hands together excitedly. "That's amazing, sweetheart. Why aren't you more excited?"

I shrug. "I guess I'm nervous." It's impossible to dampen down the guilt I feel. "It's a huge deal and could make or break my career." I toss the pancake in the pan onto a plate and add more mixture.

"Don't be nervous. You'll be amazing." The look on my mom's face is one of pure pride. It makes the guilt even harder to handle. If she knew the truth, she would be so disappointed. I try to forget about it as I flip the rest of the pancakes out onto plates and bring them over on a tray to the sofa.

"I'm sorry that I won't be around for a while," I say, glancing at my mom. "Are you going to be okay on your own?"

She digs into a pancake and shakes her head. "You worry too much. Of course, I'll be fine. Frank always comes to check up on me."

Frank is our neighbor who has always been kind to my mom. He's a good guy, but I worry about what his intentions are. He has taken a particular liking to my mom ever since he moved in two years ago. "Be careful around him, though, Mom."

She laughs. "Careful around Frank? Whatever for?"

I shake my head. "He's had a thing for you for ages."

"Nonsense, Frank doesn't have a thing for me at all." Her cheeks turn deep pink because she knows it's true.

I roll my eyes, knowing better than to argue. A comfortable silence falls between us as we eat, but I can't help the guilt eating at me. It's wrong to lie about something like this.

"Do you think I can come and watch your first performance?" Mom asks.

Fuck.

"I doubt it. The tickets are sold out, unfortunately," I lie, realizing the hole I could dig for myself right now.

"That's a shame," she says, placing the plate down on the coffee table.

"Not to mention, you need to focus on getting better at the moment." I set my plate down on the coffee table too. "Hopefully, there will be plenty of gigs for you to visit in the future."

My mom smiles. "I'm sure there will be. You're an amazing dancer."

I roll my eyes. "You have to say that because you're my mom."

She laughs. "No, it's true. The fact you landed such a high-end job proves it." She sighs. "My baby on Broadway."

Her happiness only fuels my guilt. All I can do is remind myself that I'm doing this for her. I won't sit back and do nothing when money can save her life. It's a small price to pay if it means she can fight this and live.

I GET off the bus a half-mile walk from Malachy's mansion. For a man that insists I can't go anywhere without his permission, it was shockingly easy to leave his house and go back home to see my mom.

A part of me never wanted to leave our shoddy, run-down apartment. The thought of returning to that monster's bed is enough to make me shudder.

"Hey pretty lady, wait up," a guy that had been eyeing me on the bus calls.

I quicken my pace as my stomach twists. The guy is a creep and followed me off the bus.

"Don't walk away, lass. I only want to talk." I grind my teeth, wondering if he works for Malachy. The Irish accent suggests he might. His stalking of me down the street makes me uncomfortable, particularly as it is dark. The streets are empty, and I can't call out to anyone around for help.

I swallow hard and quicken my pace, knowing I'm close to the gates of Malachy's home.

My stomach sinks when I hear his fast march turn to a run as his footsteps pound on the tarmac. I glance over my shoulder as I run, knowing the immediate danger I'm in.

The creep is too fast. I can almost feel him breathing down my neck when he finally grabs me, pulling me to a stop.

"What the fuck do you want?" I shout, yanking my arm away from him with all my strength.

He pushes me against the wall of a disused building on the right. "I told you I only wanted to talk," he says in a voice that makes me shudder.

"That's what all creeps say. My boyfriend is expecting me back any moment, and I live around the corner." I try to keep my cool. "What do you want?"

He bares his yellow teeth at me. The scent of stale liquor makes my stomach churn. He doesn't reply to my question. Instead, he gropes my ass.

Icy dread slithers through my veins as I press my hands against his chest and force him away. "Stop," I say, freeing myself. "You don't want to mess with me. My boyfriend will kill you."

It feels odd calling Malachy that. I know that if a man were to take my virginity before he had the chance, he wouldn't hesitate. The guy would be dead, and I'd be two and a half million dollars out of pocket.

The guy laughs. "I fucking doubt it. You don't know who I am."

I take a few steps away, trying to think of a plan. This guy is too large for me to fight off. Taking a stab in the dark, I decide to use his name. "Malachy McCarthy mean anything to you?"

His brow furrows. "Don't be stupid, lass. Malachy doesn't have a girlfriend."

I swallow hard. "Not a girlfriend, but he paid a high price for me." I cross my arms over my chest. "I don't think he'd be thrilled if he learned you touched me. Do you?"

His eyes narrow. "You're a liar. Malachy wouldn't give two shits what happened to a lass like you." He grabs hold of my arms again, making me shriek.

The sound of fast footsteps approaching sends relief through me. Thank God we're no longer alone.

"Shane, what the fuck are you doing, lad?"

My heart almost stops beating in my chest at the sound of Malachy's voice.

"This bitch lied and said she belongs to you. I was about to have my way with her."

I turn to face Malachy, and the recognition in his eyes quickly turns to pure rage. He doesn't direct the rage at me though.

"You fucking bastard," he growls, grabbing the guy's collar and pushing him hard against the wall he had me against a minute or two before. "You should have listened to her, Shane." The lethal warning in his voice is clear.

He punches him hard in the jaw and breaks it with one blow. The crack is sickening as the guy's jaw falls open. Malachy doesn't stop there, punching the guy who tried to rape me to a pulp. His rage is one of the most fear-inspiring things I've ever witnessed.

I slowly step away, horrified by the blood-thirsty rage Malachy has flown into. The guy was an asshole, and I've got no doubt he'd have raped me given a chance. It's hard to watch a man that I've been intimate with act so savagely. I turn away, unable to watch anymore. When the beating finally stops, I still can't bring myself to look.

Has he killed him?

It's the one question that repeats over and over in my mind. The fear of what I'd see freezes me to the spot. Malachy appears in front of me. He has blood-stains all over his white shirt and knuckles.

The frantic, almost manic look in his eyes frightens me the most. He looks wild and savage, like a man that has no idea how to be tame. "Don't say a word." There's a dangerous tone to his voice. "I want you to follow me home. Nod if you understand."

I swallow hard, feeling the fear clawing at my throat. I nod in reply, wanting nothing more than to have Malachy's intense gaze off me.

The man I've sold myself to is a maniac with violent tendencies. It's only now sunk in how much danger I'm really in.

8

MALACHY

*T*here's a tense silence as I lead Scarlett back to my room. She disobeyed me. Worse, she almost got raped by that fucking piece of scum, Shane. I have ordered my men to retrieve him and ensure he's no longer breathing.

I paid good money for the woman he almost raped, but I know that's not the reason for my questionable rage. If it had been another woman, I probably would have laughed it off. Scarlett has become coveted to me. The possession I feel when I look at her is over-whelming.

My treatment of her up to now hasn't been forceful enough. That's about to change.

I grit my teeth. I'll hate seeing that fear I saw after I'd finished beating Shane almost to death in her eyes. The way they widened when she saw the blood covering my white shirt and knuckles.

After being used to such vicious violence from a young age, it's easy to forget that most people never witness such acts. I was not that lucky. Violence has been all I've known since I was a boy.

First, my father beat me regularly, taking out his rage over my mother's death. It eased a little when he met Alicia's mother. She was a kind woman and tried her best to protect me from his rage.

I think it's why I covet my little sister. Alicia has no one but me to protect her. She is my world and always has been, even before our father and Alicia's mother died in a horrific car crash.

Once I landed in foster care with Alicia, everything went downhill. Being on the streets was easier than the foster home we got landed with.

I open the door to my room and march inside, knowing that her disobedience can't go unpunished. "Bend over the bed," I order.

Her eyes widen as she shuts the door. "What?"

I clench my bloodied fists by my side. "I said, bend over the bed."

She doesn't question me again, walking to the bed and bending over it tentatively.

I leave Scarlett waiting for me, going to the bathroom to wash the blood from my knuckles. Shane was almost dead when I finished with him. My men will finish the job and discard the evidence. I turn on the faucet and run my hands under the water, watching as it turns from clear to blood red.

Once it's all cleaned off, I pull my shirt off and toss it in the laundry basket. The lack of control I had back there in public was uncharacteristic of me.

I return to the bedroom to see Scarlett dutifully bent over the bed. The dress she has on rides up her thighs, giving me a teasing view of her lacy panties. Rage quickly turns to lust as I rub a hand across the back of my neck. I can't let her get away with this without punishment.

"You defied my orders by leaving my home. Why?" I ask.

She glances at me. "I couldn't disappear without first making up a story for my mother and going to see her."

Family again. I get the sense that this girl and I have similar values at our core. My family is everything to me. "I explicitly told you not to go home."

She returns her attention in front of her and exhales slowly. "There was no other choice."

It's not an apology. Scarlett has no intention of apologizing to me at all. "Then there is no other choice now but for me to punish you for your actions."

Her eyes widen. "Punish me how?"

I smirk, loving how delightfully innocent my little virgin is. "I think you need a good spanking. It's what all naughty, disobedient girls deserve."

Scarlett swallows and pales, staring forward again. "Fine, get it over with."

I glare at her. "What makes you think you have any

power here, darlin'?" Scarlett will learn that she does not give me orders. I grab hold of her hips hard, digging my fingertips into the bone. "I give the orders. I own you." Touching her perfectly soft skin sets mine on fire. I hate the power she inexplicably has to seduce me by doing nothing.

Shaking off the nagging doubt at the back of my mind over punishing her at all, I reach for the riding crop in the nightstand top drawer.

Scarlett is tense in front of me, waiting for her punishment.

I push the hem of her dress higher, revealing that sumptuous round ass of hers. It's enough to drive a man insane, and many would say I already am insane. "I'm going to enjoy painting your ass red, baby."

She glares at me. "Why would you enjoy doing something so sadistic?"

I shake my head. "Because the world has turned me into a twisted son of a bitch. I enjoy giving both pain and pleasure." I reach for the waistband of her panties and pull them down, revealing her perfect pussy nestled between her creamy thighs. "So beautiful," I murmur.

"You are disgusting," she says, her voice harsher than I've ever heard it.

I laugh. "I've been called worse, darlin'." I tease the tip of the leather crop over her skin softly. "You broke the rules, so don't cry when you have to get punished." I bring the crop back and hit her with moderate force on her left ass cheek. "Let this be a lesson." I do the same on her right cheek.

The second time, she cries out. "Fuck, that hurts."

I run a hand over her already stinging red skin. "I've hardly started." I run a hand through the soaking wet folds between her thighs. "You are so wet, which tells me you enjoy being punished."

"Bullshit," she says.

I bring the riding crop down harder, this time on both cheeks fast, not giving her any warning. She groans this time as if the discipline is turning her on. "Do you like that, baby girl?"

She doesn't respond to my question, keeping her eyes forward.

I strike her soft, perfect skin with the crop harder, teaching her a lesson. "I asked you a question."

"No, I don't fucking like it," she spits.

It's a lie, as her pussy has been dripping since I started. My little virgin loves being disciplined. I shove a finger into her soaking wet heat, making her moan. "Such a dirty little liar, darlin'." I spank her ass two times on either side with the crop, making her moan in pleasure. "You like being bent over like this and punished, no matter how much you try to deny it."

She groans as I slide two fingers inside of her, finding the spot that drives her crazy.

I can't help but give in to the clawing need to taste her. My tongue delves between her soaking wet lips as I lap up every drop of her. "You taste like fucking heaven, Scarlett," I growl before devouring her more.

Scarlett moans, arching her back. I lick a path from her dripping pussy up to her tight little asshole, making her tense initially. Once I do it a few more times, her moan is loud and cock-stirring. Proof that my punishment has melted her inhibitions. "Turn over so I can watch your face when I make you come," I growl.

She turns over and meets my gaze. Her stunning blue eyes are smoldering with need, which drives me insane.

I grab her thighs and delve between them, licking and sucking her like I'm an addict. Scarlett is my brand of fucking cocaine, and I can't get enough.

"I want you to come on my tongue, darlin'." I grasp her thighs harder and part them further before gently licking her throbbing clit.

"Fuck," she cries, shuddering in my hands.

"I want to taste your sweet juice as you come apart for me." I spank her right ass and then her left in quick succession. "Be a good girl and come for me."

"Yes, daddy," she cries as she comes apart.

The word startles me.

It slipped out of her accidentally, and she tenses beneath me. Her eyes are wide. "Oh, god. I'm sorry. I —" She looks like she wants to disappear as she turns a deep shade of red.

I smile down at her, despite the uncertainty over her

use of that word. A need to comfort her overwhelms me. "Don't apologize, darlin'. I'll be your daddy."

That only embarrasses her further as she shakes her head. "No, forget I said it." She tilts her head to the side, trying to avoid eye contact.

I grab hold of her throat and force her to look at me. "Don't look away, baby girl. I don't want you to be embarrassed in front of me, do you understand?"

She nods her head.

"I'm going to be the first man to fuck you. You can explore whatever dirty, hot kinks you have with me, darlin'. Nothing will shock me." It's true that nothing can shock me, but if this girl wants a Daddy Dom, I'm not sure I'm the right guy for the job.

I can't understand why a part of me even considers that role. Scarlett has darkness in her past. She's looking for someone who can help heal her, and I'm not that man. I'm too damaged myself.

She relaxes slightly, and the look in her eyes softens. It almost looks like admiration, and that worries me.

I clear my throat. "Get cleaned up," I say, nodding at the bathroom door.

She jumps up without hesitation and walks toward the bathroom. I watch after her, hating the softening I feel deep in my black heart over this vulnerable girl. The desire to protect and cherish her makes little sense. I leave the room, knowing I have to get some space from her.

Scarlett is infecting me like a disease. It's time I put some distance between us.

"Sir, how shall we strike back?"

I glance up at Niall, my second-in-command. "Find out where they are bringing in their merchandise. I need to cut them off at the source." I crack my neck, feeling irritated. The war with the Italians costs us too much. They stole a shipping container of cocaine last night from the docks, while my inept men slacked on guard. In the process, they killed four men. Maybe they've done me a fucking favor weeding out the weak and pathetic men in my operation.

The Italians have brought their drugs into the city without using the docks we run. It's a mystery how they are doing it. Milo is clever. He knows what he's doing, unlike his father, who was an idiot.

Along with these problems, I find myself distracted constantly by thoughts of the woman locked in my room. I didn't want to have to lock her in. After her blatant disregard for my orders not to see her mom and almost getting raped by one of the lowest scum in my operation, I had to take action.

It's been one week since I locked her in my room. Her slip-up with calling me daddy was oddly arousing, even though I'm not sure I could ever be that kind of Dom to her. Daddy Doms are caring, and I'm anything but. The master and slave dynamic has always suited me. Since that night, I've been toying with trying to be what she wants.

She's getting more disobedient by the day because she loves when I discipline her. Since that slip of the tongue, she hasn't called me daddy again. A part of me is disappointed.

I admire her resolve to look after her family, but I paid good money for her.

She can't be off running around while I own her. It angered me she ignored my orders, but I've ensured she's been thoroughly punished since.

A part of me had been worried about showing my true nature to the virgin I'm yet to fuck. Once I showed her my tendency for sadism, I was shocked to find her so receptive. Discipline seems to be her biggest turn-on of all.

"Sir?" Niall is staring at me with a furrowed brow. I haven't even heard a word he has said to me.

I shake my head, trying to clear my mind. "Sorry, lad. What did you say?"

Niall looks a little concerned, but he doesn't voice it to me. "I said I've got six guys trying to trace the Italian's transport route as we speak. Do you want more resources on this task?"

I rub a hand across the back of my neck as tension builds. "We can't pull too many guys off the docks after last night. Six will have to do, but I want them working fucking hard to get me my answers." I crack my knuckles. "Or else there will be hell to pay."

Niall nods. "Agreed. I'll make sure they understand how important it is."

I trust Niall like a fucking brother. He will get what needs to be done, done. It's clear that when I went into this war with Milo, I underestimated his intelligence. "Good. I think that's everything."

Niall nods and stands, lingering a moment. "Is something bothering you, sir?" His brow furrows. "You seem a little…" He either can't find the word to use or is too worried to speak frankly to me. Niall has seen the worst side of me so often but never been on the other end of my rage.

"Off?" I ask.

He nods in response. "Yeah. Not meaning any offense by it."

I draw in a deep breath and crack my neck. "The virgin I bought has been harder work than I expected. That's all."

He chuckles at that. "I'm glad I stayed the fuck away from the auction."

I give him a glare that tells him he's pushing his luck. Niall might be the best man I've got and like a brother, but I don't like being laughed at. "Normally they are easy to handle, but this girl is different."

Niall nods. "Well, be careful she doesn't get under your skin. Women can be a nightmare if they get their claws into you." Niall sounds like he's speaking from experience.

In the twenty years that I've known him, he's never had a steady relationship. He's almost as fucked up as me in many respects. "I'll give you an update as soon as we get anywhere with the Italian supply chain issue."

I watch as my right-hand man leaves me alone in the boardroom. He's a changed man from when we met. After all, we were just boys when we met on the streets. I was an up-and-coming bare-knuckle fighter, and Niall believed in me as no one else did.

He helped me train regularly. It seemed fitting that I pull him out of the streets with me when I ended up on top. Our bond is strong, even if he answers to me. Niall knows that he'd have to do something pretty fucking awful to end up dead at my hands, which means he is freer with what he says to me.

I sigh heavily and glance at the clock. It's only midday, and all my work is done. The only thing on my mind is the pretty little virgin I've yet to deflower, locked in my room and waiting for me. It's about time I take her virginity and fuck her out of my system.

9

SCARLETT

The lock on my door clicks open. A lady wearing a housekeeping uniform appears at the door. "Oh, sorry. I didn't know anyone was in here." Her brow furrows. "I need to clean the room."

I nod in reply. "No worries. I'll get out of your way for a bit," I say, eyes fixed on the door—my escape route.

She smiles. "That would be great. I won't be longer than an hour."

I grab my purse off the nightstand and slide my phone inside. "Of course, take as long as you need." The housekeeper is unaware that she freed me from captivity. It's been one week since I saw my mom. One week since he locked me in here like a caged animal. Always waiting for Malachy to come back and punish me in some sick and twisted way.

I hate that I've grown to enjoy the punishment. The

way he's so dominant and demanding. I may have sold him my virginity, but I didn't sign up for this shit. I can't stand another moment locked inside, and there's only so much dance practice I can do in this room. The mansion is quiet again, much like the day I snuck out to see my mom.

I make it to the front door, seeing no one. After what happened last time, I've no intention of leaving Malachy's grounds. I've been sitting in that fucking room staring out at the stunning grounds and woodland that runs alongside his home, longing to explore.

Malachy won't be happy if he catches me. Malachy is like clockwork and doesn't return until six in the evening each night, anyway. I'll enjoy the time of freedom I have outside and worry about Malachy later.

Another housekeeper passes me in the hall, smiling. "Morning," she says.

My heart is pounding hard at the prospect of being caught. "Morning," I reply before dashing down the stairs into the main hall. There's no one about, so I head straight out the front door—exactly how I did the other day.

When I see there's no one around outside either, my stomach settles a little. I know there's no chance I'm getting out of the gates after last time, but a walk in the fresh air will do me good.

I walk in the opposite direction of the gates and head around the back of the property. A guy in a guard's uniform with a gun walks toward me. "Morning," he says, unaware of who I am.

I nod at him. "Morning." My heart is practically pounding against my rib cage now as I head toward the woodland, hoping the cover of trees will get me away from anyone else.

Luckily, it appears no one is aware of who I am or that I shouldn't be out of the house.

I walk toward a clearing amongst the trees and head a little deeper into the woods, enjoying the shade and cover from the trees. A soft singing floats on the air toward me. A beautiful sound that almost draws me toward it. Another clearing appears, and my heart skips a beat when I see I'm not the only one in the woods.

A young lady with long brown hair has her toes dipped in a small pond and is singing so beautifully in an unfamiliar language.

I find myself mesmerized by her. It's only once she glances over and notices me that I realize the stupid mistake I made.

Her brow furrows. "Who are you?"

I swallow hard and glance back at the mansion. "My name is Scarlett, and I…" I don't even know how to explain who I am or why I'm here.

Realization dawns on her face. "Oh no, you're the newest one, aren't you?" she shakes her head. "My brother can be such a fucking pig."

My eyes widen. "Brother?"

She nods and walks toward me. "Yeah, Alicia

McCarthy. It's nice to meet you, Scarlett." She holds out her hand for me to take.

I shake it. "It's nice to meet you." I glance back toward the mansion nervously. "I'm not supposed to be outside, but I was going crazy stuck in that room."

Alicia laughs. "Don't worry. I won't tell him. My brother is amazing to me, but I know how trying he can be with most people." She glances at my arms. "You don't look as beaten up as most of the girls."

My stomach churns, and a strange jealousy twists at my gut. It's worrying to think that normally the girls Malachy buys are beaten up. What is more worrying is that thinking about him with anyone else makes me jealous.

Alicia turns her back on me and returns to the position by the lake. "Why don't you sit with me a while?"

I smile, knowing a bit of female company won't go amiss after a week locked in Malachy's room. "That would be nice." I sit down by her side. "You have a beautiful singing voice, by the way. What song were you singing?"

"Óró Sé do Bheatha 'Bhaile," she says the name of the song. "It's a Gaelic song. In English, the title is Oh, Welcome Home." She smiles wistfully. "You may not believe this, but Malachy has a beautiful singing voice too. Better than mine, even." She laughs. "Not that he ever uses it. He prefers to fight rather than sing."

I can't imagine Malachy singing. "You stayed true to your roots then, learning Gaelic?"

She nods. "Yes, my mother taught me when I was little." Her eyes grow sad. "Before she died."

I swallow hard. "Sorry to hear that. It must have been rough for you and Malachy."

She shakes her head. "Malachy loved my mother, but we are half-siblings." She sighs heavily. "I think it was easier for him once our father was gone. He abused Malachy from a young age."

I swallow hard, hearing that their father abused Malachy. It reminds me of my issues with my father. "What did he do to him?"

She doesn't look at me. "Malachy's mother died in childbirth, and our father blamed him for it. He beat him from a very young age." She shakes her head. "I shouldn't tell you all this. He would kill me if he knew."

"Don't worry. I've got no intention of telling."

Alicia smiles at me. "Thanks. I wish Malachy would stop buying women at those disgusting auctions." She gives me an apologetic look. "No offense."

"None taken." They are disgusting, but I had no other choice.

She hums the tune she had been singing softly as a comfortable silence falls between us. "Can I be rude and ask why you auctioned yourself off like that?" She tilts her head slightly. "You're not like the others."

My brow furrows. "I had no other option. My mom is sick. In what way am I different to the others?"

She claps her hands. "That explains it. All the women Malachy has purchased up to now are in it for a fancy car or nice clothes. They weren't doing it for a worthy cause." She sighs heavily. "I wish Malachy would settle down with a nice girl like you."

I feel heat filter through my body at the suggestion. There's nothing between us other than this twisted arrangement. Malachy doesn't strike me as the kind of guy who ever wants to settle down.

"Is he mistreating you?" Alicia asks, looking at me again.

I think about her question. Malachy hasn't treated me especially badly, other than the spankings. Spankings that, for some sick reason, turn me on. "Not yet." I swallow hard, wondering if the worst is to come. He hasn't even taken my virginity yet.

"What the fuck is going on here?" Malachy's voice booms.

My whole body turns to ice, and dread slices through me like a sharp blade.

Alicia, clearly not concerned by her brother's intrusion, laughs and jumps to her feet. "Malachy, I was getting to know your newest purchase. She seems nice." Alicia walks toward him and pulls him into an awkward hug.

Malachy's eyes are full of rage. "How the fuck did you get out of the room?" he asks, not acknowledging his sister.

I stand from the side of the pond. "A housekeeper came in and asked if I could give her some time while she was cleaning." I shrug. "I assumed it was fine to get some fresh air since I've been cooped up in that room for a week now."

Malachy narrows his eyes. "Alicia. Leave us." He doesn't take his eyes off of me.

"Brother, you need to chill out. Scarlett wasn't doing—"

"Alicia. I said, leave us. Don't make me ask a third time," he growls, the tone of his voice sending shivers down my spine.

Alicia gives me an apologetic look before turning around and leaving us alone in the woods.

For a few painstakingly long moments, there's silence between us. "You knew not to leave the house, but you did so anyway." He walks toward me slowly, like a wolf stalking toward a deer ready to bolt. "I can't let this disobedience go unpunished." He continues to move toward me. "What did my sister say about me?"

I shake my head. "Not much. She said you're an excellent singer."

"Bullshit," he growls. "I know my sister, and she probably gave you my life fucking story."

I swallow hard, fearing the man in front of me. After witnessing him beat a man to the brink of death, I know what he's capable of. The darkness that lies inside his soul is pure poison.

He continues to stalk toward me, forcing me to take steps backward. My heart hammers against my rib cage as I feel the hardwood of the tree behind my back. I've got nowhere to go—no escape.

Malachy towers over me as he sets a hand above me on the tree, caging me in. "What did she tell you?"

I stare into his emerald green eyes, wondering what to say. "She told me about your parents."

Malachy punches the tree above me before pacing away.

I watch as he paces in front of me with his fists clenched. "You shouldn't have come out here." I can't understand why he's so angry that Alicia told me about his past. Perhaps he prefers to be an inexcusable monster in my eyes, but I feel he's damaged because of his past.

"I'm sorry, but I was going insane in that room. I didn't sneak off the grounds. I just needed some air."

Malachy turns and glares at me. "What you need is a good punishment." He stalks toward me and pins me against the tree again. "I can't get you out of my mind, little virgin," he purrs into my ear before biting my ear lobe.

A shudder races down my spine at his declaration. "What are you going to do to me?"

He groans and kisses my neck. "So many dirty things, darlin'." He gropes my ass and lifts me, forcing me to steady myself by wrapping my legs around his waist.

"It's about time I took what I paid so much money for, but I won't be done with you once I do," he says.

My stomach clenches, and my vision blurs slightly at the prospect of Malachy fucking me here and now. I'm not ready. It's the phrase that repeats over and over in my mind. Even as my body reacts to every caress and touch from him, I know I'm not prepared mentally.

"Please, I can't—"

Malachy silences me with a kiss. A kiss that knocks the air from my lungs. It's passionate and frantic. It's the first time he's kissed me at all, and it sets my world ablaze.

I set my hands on his shoulders, feeling the need inside of me grow. All the while, my niggling doubt over being intimate with this man claws at the back of my brain.

He bites my collarbone as he thrusts a finger inside of me.

I rest my head against the tree, moaning as my nipples tighten. "Fuck."

"That's it, baby girl. I want you to come for daddy."

My heart skips a beat at the mention of the word that slipped out the other day. He looked horrified. I tense slightly, looking into his eyes.

"It's okay, darlin'. I'm going to take care of you," Malachy murmurs, kissing my neck softly. There's a tenderness in his touch that's never been there before. "I'm going to devour every inch of you and make you feel so good. You'll wish you'd sold yourself to me sooner."

I swallow hard, knowing he's not lying. Malachy has already made me experience pleasure beyond my wildest dreams. The fear over the act still cripples me. I may have gotten over the guilt of what my father made me do to him when I was so young, but I know it has scarred me permanently.

"Malachy, don't—"

He bites into my collarbone, stopping me mid-sentence.

I groan as he increases the tempo of his fingers, plunging in and out of me repeatedly. "Don't what, darlin'?" he whispers into my ear. "Don't make you come like the naughty little girl you are?"

I can no longer resist moaning at the sensation, feeling some of my reservations melt away. Malachy has a way of making me forget everything.

10

MALACHY

*H*er moans are music to my tortured soul.

Alicia shouldn't have told her about our parents. I hate people finding out how rough my life has been, as it gives them an excuse for my sick and twisted behavior. There is no excuse.

This is who I am and always will be. Dark, twisted, and tortured, but I like it that way. I'm not broken, and I sure as hell don't need mending. There was a different look in Scarlett's eyes when she looked at me, and I hated it—pity. She pities me for my past.

I keep my little virgin pinned to the tree, exploring her soft skin with my lips and teeth. Scarlett writhes in my grip, now and then half-heartedly resisting my advances.

Scarlett has darkness in her past. It's why she's unsure about intimacy, which seems a little odd considering she auctioned her virginity. Scarlett knew the moment for sex would come, and I can't wait any longer.

I slide my fingers out of her, sliding them into my mouth, tasting her. "You are going to scream while I take what I paid for right here and now."

The fear in her eyes makes me feel a little guilty. I shouldn't care if she's scared or not, but I can't help it. No matter what, I can't deny that she's special.

I slide my arms under her thighs and lift her against the tree. My desire is out of control. Control is power, and I'm losing it with Scarlett.

Scarlett grasps hold of my biceps, digging her fingertips in. "What are you going to do?"

I bite her luscious, thick bottom lip. "Fuck you, darlin'. I can't wait any longer."

She shudders, tensing against me. "I'm not sure I'm ready." There's something so vulnerable about my little virgin.

"Then you shouldn't have sold yourself to me." I nibble at the sensitive flesh at the base of her neck, making her moan softly. "I need to be inside of you." I reach for the belt around my waist, pulling it free. "I want to feel that tight little cunt wrapped around my cock."

Scarlett gasps at the use of such a dirty fucking word. Her innocence is both endearing and a turn-on. I tear her skimpy panties in two and lift the hem of her dress up.

"Please don't do this," Scarlett begs, looking into my eyes.

A part of me hesitates at her request, but it's only a small part of me. The savage and dark side of me knows that I have to claim her now. Any longer, and I'll go fucking insane—more insane than I already am.

"Sorry, baby girl, but this is what I paid for."

She closes her eyes, resting the back of her head on the tree. "Get it over with," she says, her voice cracking with emotion.

The head of my hard, throbbing cock presses against her soaking wet entrance. "I'm in control, darlin'." I bite her collarbone. "I want you to look into my eyes as I enter you."

She licks her lips nervously before opening her eyes. Those gorgeous blue gems fill with both fear and lust. She wants this, but she's scared too. It's natural, but I feel this woman doesn't know how to trust. Allowing me to enter her is the ultimate form of trust.

Too bad she doesn't have a choice. I paid two and a half million dollars for her. I won't feel bad for taking what is rightfully mine.

I lower her, so my cock is pressing hard into her tight little pussy, but not yet entering her. "You are mine, Scarlett. Mine to fuck, break, and bend however I please."

The fear in her eyes increases.

"This tight, little virgin pussy is mine. Do you understand?"

She looks into my eyes and nods. "Yes, master."

I shake my head, as it doesn't sound right. "No, baby girl. I like it when you call me daddy."

She shivers, thighs shaking violently as I hold her against the heat of my hard dick. I'm desperate to bury myself inside of her, but not until she says what I want to hear.

"Yes, daddy," she says, making my balls clench.

"Fuck, you are so perfect," I murmur into her ear before lowering her down over my shaft.

She cries out in pain initially as my huge cock stretches her tight, wet pussy for the first time. "No, please don't—" I hold her up with one arm and bring my spare hand to her throat, pinning her to the tree. "This is what you sold to me, darlin'. I'm not sure why you think you have the right to deny it to me?" My cock pulses inside of her. Desperation to fuck her hard and fast claws at me.

She looks into my eyes with a mix of lust and anger. "Because you have been toying with me for a week. It makes it more personal."

There's a sadness in her eyes, as if I've betrayed her trust by taking what is mine. I knew I was too soft with her. It's time to change that. She can't think that this is anything more than a business transaction.

"If you think there is any good in me, you're mistaken." I thrust into her slowly, fucking her against the tree. "I'm all bad, baby girl."

Her nipples are hard, pebbled peaks pointing

through the thin fabric of her dress. My dirty little virgin didn't even bother to put on a bra. I tease my hand down her chest and pull back the fabric, revealing her tight, firm breasts.

Scarlett moans as I suck on each one gently, making her pussy gush around my cock. "That's it, baby girl. I want to hear you moan for me."

"Fuck," she cries as I pound into her harder.

All reasoning is gone as I fuck her, desperate to make her mine in every sense of the word.

Her fingertips claw into my arm as I continue to fuck her harder and faster. The savage inside of me has broken free, and there is no stopping me now.

"Oh, fuck, yes," Scarlett cries, arching her back in a way that allows me to sink even deeper inside of her.

I grunt, biting her collarbone as I fuck her harder. It's a shock that my dirty little virgin can take it so roughly. This position isn't ideal for fucking her hard, so I carry her from the tree still embedded on my cock and find a small patch of grass to lower her to.

"You are fucking perfect, baby girl." I groan as I memorize the image of her right here and now. Scarlett looks like an angel with her swollen, hard nipples and dripping wet pussy wrapped around my cock, lying on the soft grass.

Scarlett stares into my eyes, and it feels like she can see right into my soul. It makes me feel vulnerable. I kiss her lips softly and tease my tongue against them, seeking entrance.

She obliges, allowing me to kiss her deeply. Our tongues tangle together in a dance of passionate lust for one another.

I can sense how much she wants me. It seems our souls long for each other for some inexplicable reason. It's a profound connection that I've never felt with another human being, and it scares me. Few things scare me in this world, but Scarlett is an enigma.

I kiss a path down her neck, keeping my hard, throbbing cock deep inside of her. Slowly, I move in and out of her. Each thrust harder than the last as I make her writhe beneath me.

"Oh, yes," she cries, arching her back more. "Harder," she orders.

I growl softly and tease my hand around her neck, blocking her airways a little. "Who's in charge, baby girl?"

She bites her bottom lip. "You are, sir."

I grind my teeth together, wondering why I so badly want her to call me daddy. It's not in my nature to be caring, and yet I want to care for her. I want to protect her and keep her safe. I don't push the matter. If she thinks I'm letting her go after I've taken her virginity, she is wrong. Scarlett is mine for as long as I want.

I let go of her throat and fuck her even harder and faster, pounding into her like a wild animal.

There's something primal and natural about fucking outside. I've never done it before, as I'm always in control. When I saw Scarlett outside, my rage, coupled with my insatiable desire to have her, broke my control. I had to fuck her here and now.

"I can't get enough of you," I whisper against her lips before digging my fingertips into her hips and pounding even harder into her.

"Fuck, Malachy," she cries.

The sound of my name from her lips drives me crazy. "Call my name, baby girl. I can't wait to feel that heavenly pussy come on my cock," I growl.

I'm sure all the guards can hear us fucking in the woods, but I don't give a shit. All I care about is making the woman beneath me mine. I never want another man to touch her. She's mine forever since I claimed her first.

It's crazy since I know that this sick and twisted arrangement will end. I bought Scarlett's virginity, not her. Keeping her captive forever would only make her hate me, but it's a tempting fucking thought.

I've never let what someone else wants get in the way of my needs. Although, this is a different scenario entirely.

"Malachy, I think I'm going to—"

I kiss her, knowing what she's going to say. The muscles around my cock tighten and pulse as she comes undone. "That's it, baby girl. Come on my cock," I purr against her lips, groaning as my release rushes closer.

I want to fill her with my seed until it's dripping down her thighs.

"Oh, yes," she cries, as her juices gush around my

cock. Her pussy is so tight around me I can't fight the release any longer.

I thrust into her hard three more times before exploding inside of her. I keep thrusting, releasing every drop from my balls. "That's it, darlin'. I'm going to fill you with my cum, so every man knows you belong to me," I growl.

She tenses slightly at the sentiment, but I don't care. Scarlett is mine whether or not she wants to be.

I rest inside of her for a short while, listening to her frantic breathing. We're silent together, but it's not awkward. There are no words that need to be said right now.

Slowly, I roll off her and pull her against my chest, staring up at the dappled canopy of leaves above us.

Scarlett doesn't pull away, resting her head on my still clothed chest. I never hold a woman after fucking her, but then I've never wanted a woman the way I want Scarlett.

It's a dangerous notion, but one that is truer than even I can comprehend.

11

SCARLETT

*I*t's been a week since Malachy took my virginity so roughly in the woods. He hasn't mentioned letting me go yet. Even though he has taken what he paid for, he has no intention of letting me out of this earlier than one or two months, as originally stated.

I can't believe what I've been missing out on all this time, held back by my crippling fears. Sex with Malachy is better than I ever could have imagined, and despite his rough and savage ways, Malachy makes me feel wanted. The way he looks at me makes me feel cherished.

The way he held me as we lay in the woods, for God knows how long, was possessive and protective. He may be dark and dangerous, but he can be caring too.

I jolt as someone clears their throat behind me as I sit on the garden bench close to the mansion. I turn around and see Malachy looking at me with a mix of adoration and hesitation.

"Hey, what's up?" I ask, smiling at the man who has inexplicably torn down some of my walls.

He smiles and sits down next to me. "Nothing. I was looking for you, darlin'." He takes my hand in his and looks out over the lush lawns.

I can't help but believe that he's lying. "Are you sure?"

He glances over at me, revealing the dominant side of him I crave. "Don't question me, baby girl."

I bite my lip, feeling heat pool between my thighs at the tone of his voice. A voice in my head says, *Sorry, daddy,* but I can't bring myself to call him that again.

I shocked myself when it came out the first time, unsure why it did. It makes no sense. A deep part of me wants to revert to the childhood that was stolen from me. Malachy makes me feel safe despite the danger surrounding him and his savage and dominant ways.

"What are you thinking?" he asks.

I shake my head. "Not much." I feel the heat rising through my chest and neck, as I can't tell him. It reveals too many secrets about my screwed-up past.

"Tell me," he orders.

I swallow hard, feeling my walls closing in on me at the sudden harshness in his tone. "I wasn't thinking of anything in particular," I say, not looking him in the eye.

Malachy grasps my throat in that dominant way, making my stomach churn. "Bullshit. You were blushing." He moves his face within an inch of mine. "I want to know every dark and dirty thought that enters that precious little mind of yours, darlin'."

I look into his striking green eyes, and my uncertainty eases. There's no explanation for why I want to bare my soul to this man. He makes me want to break down the walls, but I'm scared he will crush my heart if I do. The walls are my safety net. They've been there for as long as I can remember.

"I was thinking about why I have the urge to call you daddy all the time," I murmur, holding his gaze as the heat increases in my face.

He smiles the most handsome smile. "Because I make you feel safe, even if I am the last person who should make you feel that way."

I raise a brow. "Why?"

He shrugs. "Might have something to do with the fact I'm the leader of the Irish mafia, or that I'm the undefeated bare-knuckle champion of Boston." He lets go of my throat, chuckling slightly. "I mean, you've witnessed me almost kill a man with my bare hands. I'm dangerous."

The memory of him beating that guy in front of me makes me shudder. Perhaps that's why he makes me feel safe. He didn't hesitate to beat him to a pulp for almost raping me. I feel he would do anything to protect me, which has a power over me.

I bite my lip and shake my head. "You're not dangerous to me," I breathe.

He holds my gaze, searching my eyes as if he's searching for the answer to a question in them. "No, because I'll protect you with my life." He leans toward me and kisses me tenderly. "You're mine now, Scarlett, and no one dares to harm what is mine."

I lock my hands behind his neck and kiss him more deeply, feeling the passion of his promise in our kiss.

He breaks it and tilts his head to the side slightly. "I told you that you could call me whatever you want. Why did you stop?"

I glance down at my hands in my lap. "It feels a little weird to call you that." I feel my throat close up, as it's such a confusing word to me. My father was abusive and not the kind of man that made me feel safe. Perhaps I'm craving that from Malachy as he's the first man who has made me feel cherished, even if he is rough and dangerous.

"Tell me why it feels weird." It's not a question but a demand, although I know that I'm not ready to tell him about my past.

I reach for the back of his neck and pull him close, but he resists.

"Don't distract me."

I shake my head. "I'm not ready to tell you."

His jaw clenches, and he nods, although I can tell it frustrates him. "I understand, but I want to know everything about you eventually, darlin'," he murmurs, pulling me close to him. "Now, the real reason I came to find you is that I wanted to ask you out to dinner tonight."

My brow furrows as I stare at the rough, gorgeous Irish man I can feel myself slowly falling for. "Like a date?"

He shrugs. "If you want to call it that."

I look out over the lawn and watch as a bird swoops down and catches a worm, flying back up into the sky. A date with Malachy changes the entire dynamic. Up to now, although he has made me feel protected, this has been nothing more than a business transaction. I can't understand why dinner with him makes me nervous, especially after everything we've done together.

"What do you say?" he asks.

I meet his expectant gaze. "Dinner would be nice, but..." I wonder how to go about asking the next question.

"What is it, Scarlett?" he asks, setting a hand on my thigh. The touch of his skin against mine sets me on fire.

I meet his gaze again. "How long do you think you will continue to keep me here?"

There's a flash of anger in his eyes at the question. "As long as I desire."

I swallow hard, wondering if I can have any feelings for a man sick enough to buy a virgin at auction. According to his sister, I'm far from the first. A man who had no reservations about locking me in his room for a week and using me for his every whim and desire.

Not to mention, I don't have any say when I get away from him.

"On second thought, I think it's best we keep this strictly professional. No dinner." I shake my head.

Malachy growls and grabs hold of my throat so hard it's almost impossible to breathe. "It's not a question. It may have seemed like one, but you do as I say when I say. Do you understand?"

I nod in reply.

He tightens his grip on my throat. "Let me hear you say it."

It's crazy the way this conversation changed so suddenly. "Yes, sir."

His eyes narrow. "That's not what I wanted to hear, baby girl, and you know it."

I grind my teeth together. "Yes, master."

The growl that comes from him is so animalistic I wonder if a bear wandered into the grounds. "Call me daddy," he demands.

Wetness pools between my thighs at the word, and my nipples harden. He doesn't deserve the title when he acts like this. "Yes, daddy," I say quietly, knowing he won't let go until he's heard me say it.

He lets go of my throat, and I gasp for air. "Good. I want you ready for dinner at seven o'clock. I've made reservations." He stands and turns his back on me.

I watch as he walks away stiffly, feeling so torn inside.

On the one hand, Malachy makes me feel safe—

safer than I've felt before. It appears all this time, deep down, I've craved a protector who can shield me from all the shit this world offers.

When I look into Malachy's eyes, it's like looking into a mirror. He's damaged, but he's also a protector. The kind of man that will do anything to keep his possessions safe, and it makes being his possession alluring.

On the other hand, I have no say over anything. He may make me feel safe, but when he comes to ask me to dinner, it's not a question but a demand.

I don't have a choice.

I've fallen prey to the promise of safety from him. It's all I've craved for as long as I can remember. The question is, can anyone truly be safe around a man as dangerous as Malachy McCarthy?

12

MALACHY

I glance at the clock on the wall as the large hand moves to four. Three hours until I return to my house to collect Scarlett for dinner.

Our conversation was going so well until she rejected my offer for dinner. I snapped when she told me she wouldn't come.

I think it's best we keep this strictly professional.

Her words replay over and over like a broken record. To her, this is a business transaction and nothing more. It should be the same for me, but she's made me care for her. I think the moment she stepped onto that stage, I knew she was different.

Niall knocks on the door to my office. "Sir, can I come in?"

I nod in reply.

He enters and sits opposite me. "We've worked out how the Italians are bringing in their product."

I sit up straighter, smirking. "Perfect. I hope we can intercept."

Niall doesn't look too sure. "They're bringing in product to the docks at Salem."

My brow furrows. "Are you serious?" I shake my head. "We can't block them without pissing off the Russians." I run a hand across the back of my neck.

Mikhail Gurin owns the docks in Salem. If we were to intercept the Italian's haul there, then we would be in serious trouble with the Russians too. We could never survive a war on two fronts against the Russians and the Italians.

"How do they get the drugs into the city?" I ask.

Niall sighs heavily. "Haulage trucks, but we can't seem to find a pattern in their routes. Every route they take is different." He runs a hand across his jaw. "The Italians aren't stupid. They know they have to be careful at the moment."

I slam my fist on the table before standing and pacing my office. Milo Mazzeo is one clever son of a bitch, unlike his stupid, hothead of a father. The guy was easier to read than a book, and I'd hoped Milo would be the same.

"How are we going to strike back if they keep one step ahead of us all the time?" I ask, glancing at my right-hand man.

He shrugs. "I don't know, sir. It seems like everything we think of, they've already taken precautions to stop."

I inhale a deep breath, trying to clear my mind. It doesn't help that every minute of every day, Scarlett consumes my thoughts. Normally, I'm the brains behind the operations, but I can hardly think straight.

"Niall, I need you to help me out here, lad. I'm coming up blank."

He scrubs a hand across the back of his neck. "Maybe we don't hit his supply." There's a glint in his eyes that tells me he has a wicked plan. "The supply is only the start of the chain. Why don't we fuck up his laundering? That way, he can't clean any of his cash."

I smile at him, shaking my head. "You bloody genius." I laugh. "I've been so set on cutting off the supply. I hadn't even thought about the chain." I walk over to him and clap his shoulder. "That's why you are my second. Now, get that plan in motion with the guys and report back to me once done."

He nods. "Aye, sir, on it." He stands and leaves me alone with my messy thoughts. I would have thought of a plan in normal circumstances, but I'm a train wreck at the moment. The reason is the fiery redhead who has me twisted up inside.

Scarlett has infected me like a disease—a disease that is slowly spreading the longer I have her around. I feel like I'm at a crossroads, and the next step I take will change my life forever.

The ultimate question is, what is my next move?

I'M NOT sure why I'm so hung up on looking after Scarlett. Her desire for a protector has dictated my treatment of her. Normally, I would be happy to break my purchases, but I've handled Scarlett with more care.

There's something different about her I can't quite put my finger on. All I know is that I don't want to let her go in one, two, or three months. She's my addiction and fucking her didn't help. It made my obsession with her worse.

My heart is pounding frantically against my rib cage. I don't do dating. The maid gave me a strange look when she saw me all dressed up and holding a bouquet. This isn't me, yet I feel this odd longing to satisfy Scarlett's desire for a man who can care for her.

I open the bedroom door, and the breath is knocked from my lungs. Scarlett is sitting on the edge of the bed, wearing a stunning silver dress that accentuates her curves. "Fuck, you look stunning," I say, walking toward her.

Scarlett looks up, meeting my gaze. Her eyes travel down my body, taking in my navy-blue suit. "You don't look bad yourself," she says, eyes dilating with a desire that makes it hard not to toss her onto the bed and have my way with her. Right now, all I'm hungry for is Scarlett.

"If you talk like that, we might never make our dinner reservation." I kiss her cheek. "These are for you." I place the bouquet in her hand.

She licks her bottom lip in a way that drives me

insane, standing finally. It gives me an even better view of the dress she is wearing. "Thank you," she says, placing them on the bed.

I grab her hips hard, pulling her close. "You look so tempting. I wouldn't mind fucking you right here and now."

Scarlett shudders. "Do we have time?"

I smile at my eager little virgin. She can't get enough now that I've finally made her realize what she has been missing. "Do you want me to fill you with cum so you can feel it dripping into your panties while we eat dinner?"

Scarlett's eyes widen. "You wouldn't—"

I grab hold of her throat and push her against the wall of the bedroom. "Don't challenge me, darlin'." I kiss a path up her exposed neck. "I would and will now."

Her eyes are filled with a mix of fear and lust. I know she fears me when I lose control, but I have no way of gaining control when it comes to her. A primal need to make her mine and make her submit rules me all the time.

I bite her bottom lip softly, making her moan. "I'm going to fuck you hard and fast against the wall and fill you with my seed." I bite her exposed collarbone, leaving a mark. "I want my mark on you wherever you go, so every man knows you belong to me."

She shudders again as I move my hands under the

skirt of her dress and gently caress her soft thighs. "Malachy, please—"

I growl softly and press my lips to hers. "Don't speak, or I'll bend you over my knee. I'm in control, darlin'." I slip a finger into her panties before tearing them apart. "I'm going to fuck this tight little cunt whenever I want." I slip a finger inside of her and groan at how wet she is. "Always so wet and ready for my cock, aren't you, Scarlett?"

She bites her lip and shakes her head. "No."

"Fucking liar, baby girl. You're practically dripping for me."

I unbuckle my belt with the other hand and then free my cock, fisting it in my hand. "You are gagging for my cock, admit it."

Her eyes dilate as she takes in my size, licking her lip. "I am. Give it to me," she purrs.

I smirk. "Ask nicely, baby girl."

Her back arches, and she moans. "Give me your cock, please, daddy."

My cock leaks cum onto the floor, and I can no longer wait. I slide my arms under her knees and lift her against the wall. "We don't have much time, darlin'. I'm going to fuck you so hard and fast they will hear you scream in central Boston."

Scarlett shivers. Her expression is pure lust now as she stares me straight in the eye. "Yes, please," she mutters, driving me insane.

I lower her fast and thrust my cock hard into her

tight little pussy. The way her muscles grip me is heaven.

"Yes, Malachy," she cries as I thrust into her hard and fast, not giving her a chance to get used to my size.

I'm a beast, and I've lost control. The need to devour her is all that fuels me. I bite her shoulder hard enough to hurt as I hold her weight, thrusting into her with no reserve. I'm like an animal rutting. All that matters is making us both come as hard and fast as physically possible.

Scarlett's arms remain locked around my neck as she helps me hold her. I bite her neck softly, making her moan so loud. "Fuck, daddy, you are going to make me come," she cries.

I chuckle against her skin. "That's the intention, baby girl. I want you to come so hard on my cock."

She cries out again, arching her back so much that I slide even deeper—as deep as physically possible. My cock is practically buried to the balls in her tight little pussy.

"Yes, daddy," she screams as I feel her muscles spasm around my cock. A gush of sweet juice floods around my shaft as she comes undone. The pressure of her muscles clamped around my cock is too much to bear as I come apart too. I empty load after load of my seed deep inside of her, thrusting repeatedly until I'm sure she's full to the brim.

Once I've finished, I carry her to the bed and lower her down on her back. "Don't move."

She looks up at me quizzically, her brow furrowed.

I walk into the closet and grab a pair of basic, thick cotton panties.

Scarlett looks even more confused as I return with them. "What are you doing?"

I don't answer her and pull the torn panties off her. Slowly, I slip the other panties on and make sure they're tightly fitted. "I want to keep my cum inside of you the best I can."

Scarlett's cheeks redden. "It won't stay in there. It will just seep into the fabric."

I spank her thigh. "Don't be smart with me, darlin'. It will help. I love the idea of sitting opposite you in the restaurant, knowing my cum is still inside of you." I lift her from the bed and set her on her feet, spanking her firm ass cheeks gently. "Now come on, we're going to be late because you're such a dirty little girl."

I grab Scarlett's hand and pull her toward the door, knowing deep down that I've got it bad for not being able to resist her before dinner. Scarlett is under my skin, and I know I can't get her out.

13

SCARLETT

*M*alachy's gaze is intense as he watches me from across the table.

I feel more confused than ever. Malachy turned up at the door dressed impeccably in a suit with flowers, as if he were ready to be a gentleman. First, he asked me to dinner and then turned up so well dressed. It didn't last long, though, as he fucked me like a savage and made sure he filled me with his cum for our dinner date. It makes me feel so dirty as I clench my thighs together.

I remember the way he savagely grabbed my throat and pinned me against the wall. It's not the first time he has handled me like that, but it was the harshest he's been with me. I feel that I've only seen a tame side of Malachy.

"I hope you like Italian food. This is the best Italian place in town."

I nod in response. "Yes, I do." There's an awkward tension between us ever since we arrived.

A waiter approaches, looking at Malachy strangely. "Are you sure you should be here, Mr. McCarthy?"

He cracks his neck. "What the fuck is that supposed to mean?"

The waiter pales. "It's just that Mr. Mazzeo isn't too pleased." He glances toward another table near the back where a suave-looking man sits, staring down at us angrily.

He's with a beautiful, dark-haired woman.

Malachy waves his hand. "It's a free fucking country, and I wanted Italian food. Now bring me the best bottle of Prosecco you've got."

The waiter glances at the man at the back before reluctantly nodding. "Of course, sir."

"Bloody Italians," Malachy murmurs once he's walked away.

"Do you know that man?" I ask, nodding toward the table where the guy is still glaring at us.

Malachy glances over and nods. "We're currently at war with him."

I raise a brow. "War?"

He lets out a frustrated sigh. "Yes, we had a disagreement. I don't want to talk about work."

"I assume he owns this restaurant. Isn't it a stupid idea to come here if you are at war with him?"

Malachy laughs. "No, the bastard wouldn't dare try something here. It's too public, baby girl." He reaches for my hand across the table, but I move it away. A flash of anger pulses through his bright green eyes. Instead of acknowledging my reluctance to touch him, he focuses his attention on the menu. "What are you going to order?"

I've hardly looked at the menu, but I know there's only ever one thing I order at an Italian restaurant, and that's lasagna. "Lasagna, if it's on the menu."

Malachy meets my gaze. "Me too. It's my favorite."

My stomach flips at his admission of loving lasagna too. I break our eye contact and turn my attention to the menu, making sure there's nothing else I want. "I'll get a side of garlic bread too."

The waiter returns with the champagne and two glasses. "Are you ready to order?"

Malachy nods. "Yes, two lasagnas and two sides of garlic bread, please."

The waiter notes it down and hurries away from our table.

"It seems like the waiter fears you," I point out.

He nods. "Quite right. He should be scared." He pours us each a glass of Prosecco, cursing under his breath at the shit service here. Once finished, he passes me a glass. "A toast to us."

My brow furrows. "To our business agreement, you mean."

His eyes narrow. "No, baby girl. To us."

I swallow hard at the intensity in his voice. There is no *us*, but I feel it's not the best time or place to argue. Instead, I sip the champagne and keep my mouth shut.

It's become clear ever since I met the dangerous Irish don that he's a little unhinged. There is no doubting that we have a connection and chemistry unlike any I've experienced before, but he bought me for fuck's sake.

Whatever this is, it can't turn into something real. Not after the way it started.

"Tell me about your family," Malachy says, an order again rather than a question.

I shrug. "Not much to tell. My mom is all the family I have in this world, and that's why I entered the auction to ensure I can help her fight her illness."

Malachy doesn't look pleased with my answer. "Where is your father?"

My spine stiffens at the mention of him. "Out of the picture." I don't want to tell him the truth. My father is still in prison, as far as I'm aware. He has constantly been in and out of jail for assaulting minors. The man is sick in the head.

Malachy clicks his tongue. "What happened between your father and mother? I want to know, Scarlett."

I clear my throat and meet his gaze. "Why?" I ask, infusing my tone with as much confidence as I can muster.

I can't see why he needs to know this information.

The only reason I can think of is to use it against me. I won't let him do that.

The waiter returns with our food, breaking the thick tension between us. "Thank you," I say as he sets the lasagna down in front of me. The scent is divine and makes my stomach rumble.

Once he's gone, Malachy clears his throat. "Scarlett, remember who owns you. You don't question me. Answer the question."

I shake my head. "You purchased my virginity, which you have already taken. You don't own me. No one does," I say, holding my head up high and taking a bite of the delicious lasagna.

Malachy's eyes flash with wild rage as he slams his fist down on the table. "You're heading the right way for a good punishment. I'll pull you over my knee right here and spank you raw."

I can't understand why my thighs quiver at the thought.

"Sorry to interrupt, but I had to welcome you to my restaurant, Malachy." The man who owns the place stands next to me, his hand on the back of my chair.

I notice Malachy's jaw tick as his eyes zero in on how close his enemy is standing to me.

"Milo. What the fuck do you want?"

He shakes his head. "That isn't a very nice way to speak to the owner of the restaurant you are eating at, is it?" There's cold confidence in his voice that sends shivers through me. "Who do we have here then?" he asks, towering over me.

"Leave her alone, Milo," Malachy says, his voice more lethal than I've heard it before.

Suddenly, the danger of this situation hits me. Two mafia dons that are at war with each other are facing off, and I'm caught in the middle.

"What is your name, bella?" Milo asks.

I swallow hard. "Scarlett," I say, holding out a hand to him to defuse the tension. "It's very nice to meet you."

He smiles at me, but it's not a friendly smile at all. It's cruel and cold. "Indeed," he says, taking my hand and pressing his lips to the back of it. "At least you have some manners, not that the same can be said for your date."

Malachy growls and stands to his feet, squaring up to Milo. "Why don't you run along and get back to your pretty little wife. If we weren't in public, I don't think you would approach me like this, you fucking coward, not after last time."

Milo's jaw clenches as he stares into Malachy's eyes.

My heart is pounding so hard I'm surprised everyone can't hear it. I wonder what happened last time. Malachy continues. "If you want a rematch, I'd happily pummel you to a pulp this time if you don't run away like a bitch," he snaps.

Milo lifts his jacket to reveal a pistol at his belt.

"Don't think I won't shoot you dead right here and now, McCarthy."

Malachy laughs. "You don't have the balls." He pulls up his jacket to reveal a gun and the hilt of a knife. "Plus, I'd slit your throat open before you had a chance." He shakes his head. "I wouldn't have come here if I'd have known you'd be here. I just wanted some fucking Italian food, even if I hate Italians."

Milo steps back, and it's the first sign of either of them backing down. "Fine. I'll leave you in peace, but don't come here again. There are other Italian restaurants in this city that I don't own." He turns around and smiles at me. "You are too good for him, bella." He walks past me and returns to the table at the back of the restaurant.

I watch as Malachy sits down, but the manic rage in his eyes doesn't disappear. I realize I could end up on the wrong end of that rage now.

Malachy meets my gaze. "Fucking Italians." He shakes his head. "I shouldn't have brought you here."

I tilt my head to the side. "Why did you if there are other restaurants we could have gone to?"

He shrugs. "Research and dinner. I wanted to kill two birds with one stone. My second-in-command, Niall, needed some intel on this place."

My stomach sinks the moment I learn the true reason for this dinner. Malachy didn't only invite me to dinner because he wanted to get to know me. He invited me as an excuse to do some digging. It hurts more than I can explain. The feelings I have for this man make no sense.

"How is the lasagna?" he asks.

I shrug. "It's good, but I've lost my appetite."

Malachy signals over the waiter. "Can I get the food to go and the check, please?"

The waiter nods, clearing the plates to package the food up.

I'm thankful that I don't have to be here any longer. Milo, the owner of the place and Italian don, is even more unnerving the Malachy. There's something lethal about him.

"What happened last time?" I ask.

Malachy's brow furrows. "What?"

I nod toward Milo's table. "With Milo. What happened last time?"

His throat bobs as he stares into my eyes. "It doesn't matter."

It's rich that he expects me to open up about the most intimate details of my dark past, but he can't even tell me about the last time he met with his enemy. It's clear that his opinion is this only goes one way. I tell him what he wants, but he keeps me at arm's length.

I won't answer any more of his questions, as I know it can only lead to heartache. My heart has been on the line with this man ever since he took my virginity. I know that if I carry on down this path, I won't survive him.

14

MALACHY

*S*carlett sits at a distance from me in the back of the cab, staring out of the window.

I saw the hurt in her eyes when I told her our dinner was my attempt to scope out an enemy's restaurant.

After I refused to tell her what happened between Milo and me when we last met, she has barely looked at me. She doesn't need to know that I assaulted his wife with a knife, shot his right-hand man, and beat him up before they escaped.

There is one fact with me, I'm fiercely loyal to my family and friends, but I'm savagely vicious with my enemies. Nothing is off the table with my opposition, and that's something many people can't comprehend— the depths of my depravity when dealing with people who cross me.

Milo isn't much different. He's cold, calculating, and he does what needs to be done. I think it's why we clash so much. We both do whatever's necessary to win, but there can never be two winners.

The difference between Milo and me is that he has no family and nothing to lose except for his new wife. I'm not sure what their relationship is truly like since it was an arranged marriage.

I keep my family a closely guarded secret, hence why Milo stupidly killed my backstabbing cousin, unaware of who he was to me.

I glance at the beautiful red-haired beauty I purchased just over two weeks ago at the last auction. It hits me at that moment that Scarlett is another person I've got to lose. This time, my stupidity means Milo knows her. Sure, he doesn't know who she is to me or if she's important. To be honest, neither do I.

There was a dark glint of amusement in that sick son of a bitch's eyes as he looked at my girl. The fact is, she is mine. I have no intention of ever letting her go, even if she believes she'll be free in a couple of months.

"You didn't answer me in the restaurant," I say, forcing her to look at me. Her stunning, bright blue eyes look sad.

"What?" she asks, looking puzzled.

I narrow my eyes. "I asked you what happened between your father and mother?"

She shakes her. "Not much. They split up."

I know she's lying to me. There's darkness in her past that she won't reveal, and it's driving me crazy.

"You're lying. What did your father do to you, baby girl?"

I see the barriers erecting as she tenses, moving further away from me. She's practically pressed against the cab door as if trying to blend into it. "Nothing," she says, her voice small and timid.

"He hurt you, didn't he?" I feel rage at the thought of a man who is supposed to care for and protect her, hurting her. "Is that why you and your mother left?"

Her brow furrows, and she meets my gaze. "Why do you care?" she snaps. Rage is her go-to emotion when pushed, just like me. "I don't ask you questions about your father abusing you."

It feels like she has kicked me in the gut. Damn Alicia and her big fucking mouth. I should have known she'd tell her more than just the story of our parent's death. I grab hold of her throat and look into her eyes. "How much did Alicia tell you? And I want the truth this time."

Scarlett glares back at me. "Just that your father blamed you for your mother dying giving birth to you and was abusive."

I let go of her throat and growl softly. "I hate people knowing the truth, as it makes me look weak. I'm not weak. My father's beatings made me the man I am today, and I'm glad of it."

Scarlett watches me carefully, fear in her eyes. "Why would you be glad your father abused you?" Her brow furrows.

"Whenever anyone hears the fucking sob story of my life, they always pity me and think that it's the reason I'm the way I am. I'm not broken." I search Scarlett's eyes, wondering if she feels the same about whatever shit she went through. "I like the person I am, and I have no fucking desire to be any different. Violence is a part of me I wouldn't change for the world. I don't care if that makes me a maniac or psychopath or whatever you want to call me."

She nods slowly. "I guess that makes sense." She swallows hard, looking into my eyes and searching them for a few moments. "My father made me do stuff to him from as early as I can remember until my mother walked in on it when I was eight years old."

Rage slams into me, hard. "What things?" I growl.

She looks ashamed as she stares down at her hands. "He used to make me get him off." Scarlett shakes her head. "I don't want to talk about it."

I grab hold of her chin and make her look me in the eye. "Never feel ashamed. You've got nothing to be ashamed of. That bastard that should have looked after you, lass." I can feel the rage infecting my veins. "Please tell me he is dead, or I will have to hunt him down and slit his throat single-handedly."

Her eyes widen, and she shakes her head. "He's not dead, but I think he's back in jail after assaulting a seven-year-old girl, last I heard."

It makes me so mad to hear that the man that was supposed to be the only man she could trust in the world was the opposite. He doesn't deserve to be breathing. To top it off, he's fucking with other kids. There's nothing worse in this world than a man who gets off sexually abusing children.

"How did your mother find out?" I ask, wanting to hear if she had any hand in this.

Scarlett swallows hard, a haunted look in her eyes as if she's being transported back. "She was sick and sent home early from her shift at work. My mom walked in on it happening, called the police, and moved us up to Boston from Texas where he could never find us again." She shakes her head. "He got sentenced to ten years but was out in five."

"Bullshit justice system. I bet he's been in and out all of his life, hasn't he?"

Scarlett nods in response. "I put that part of my life behind me, but it feels like he stole my childhood from me."

I know that feeling all too well. My father stole my childhood from me the moment he hit me for the first time. All my life I've fended for myself.

I feel a sense of pride that Scarlett felt comfortable enough to call me daddy. It means she feels safe with me, something I've taken for granted. "I'm sorry, baby girl." I kiss her lips. "Don't worry. I'm going to make sure that man can't touch another child ever again."

She tenses. "What are you going to do?"

I shake my head. "Don't worry about it. You're safe with me, I promise." I run a hand through her fiery red hair, feeling the need to care for her ignite stronger inside of me. "I'll protect you no matter the cost."

She looks up at me with wide eyes. "Why would you protect me?"

I clench my jaw, uncertain of the answer to that. "Because you're mine." I feel Scarlett shake against me at my possessive declaration of ownership. "You know I don't like being questioned, baby girl." I kiss her again. "Perhaps I need to punish you."

Scarlett bites her bottom lip. "I did nothing wrong, though," she says.

I smirk at her. "Don't talk back and do as daddy says."

Her eyes dilate, and she shuffles in her seat, clearly hot over the idea of being punished. "Sorry, daddy," she murmurs, making my cock harder than nails.

I wrap my hand around the back of her neck and lean in close. "You will be once I have my way with you, darlin'." I kiss her passionately, allowing her to feel the intensity of my desire for her.

Scarlett moans into my mouth as our tongues tangle. There's such raw emotion between us. An emotion I didn't know I had the capability of feeling until I met her. My damaged angel needs a man who can protect and cherish her. Although it's not in my nature, I feel inclined to oblige.

I want to keep hold of this one as long as possible and giving her what she desires will make it easier.

I WATCH as my angel walks into the room, placing her hand on the comforter and running her fingers through the soft, plush fabric.

There's a tension between us. It's been building ever since I told Scarlett the truth, and she told me about her past. Her father's abuse angers me. Sure, my father beat me when I was younger, but the sick son of a bitch who was supposed to cherish Scarlett violated her in worse ways at such a young age.

I'm glad she told me, as I've already informed Niall to find him. There's no way I'm letting that man live after what he did to her. Once I get my hands on him, he'll wish he had never been born.

She's hurting from her past. I'm not sure I'm the right man to help her heal, but I want to try. Anyone with sense would tell her to run and never look back. My life is dangerous and so am I. I'm ruled by one emotion I can never rid myself of—anger. Anger that I never want to take out on Scarlett.

"Are you okay, baby girl?" I ask.

She glances over at me, and the only thing I see in her eyes is unadulterated desire. "Yes, daddy," she murmurs, making me groan.

I'd never given a thought to the daddy and little dynamic, but if it's what she's into, then I'm willing to give it a go. "Do you want to be my little girl, Scarlett?"

Scarlett blushes a deep red, making my cock harder. "I don't know. What does that mean?"

Her innocence is sexy. I walk toward her and take a seat on the sofa. "Sit down," I order.

She hesitates a moment before sitting down by my side.

"It means you act younger than you are, submitting to me as the dominant figure in your life. You call me daddy whenever we're role-playing." I watch her reactions. "If you are naughty, then I punish you." I shrug. "It's not something I've considered before, and I'll be as new to it as you. I'm normally into more hardcore BDSM." I can't understand why I'm changing my preferences for this girl. Master and slave was always my go-to role. "Normally, I lean toward master and slave roles."

Scarlett's eyes widen slightly. "That's why you asked me to call you master?"

I nod. "Yes, but the daddy and little relationship is more caring."

She glances down at her hands as she plays with them nervously in her lap. "Why would you change what you normally do when you paid so much money for me?"

It's a good fucking question, one I can't find the answer to. "Because you need a caregiver. A man you can trust, and I won't be the one to steal that from you. I want to give it to you instead."

Her cheeks flush an even darker red, driving me crazy.

"Although, it would mean you'd have to trust me and give me your submission."

Scarlett looks away again, staring down at her hands. "I don't know how to."

I lift her chin and force her to meet my gaze. "I can teach you." I press my lips to hers. "I can show you how good pleasure and pain mixed can be."

She shivers. "Pain?"

I meet her gaze again. "Yes, when you are a naughty girl and don't do as daddy says, I will have to punish you."

Scarlett shudders as I hold her hand. "How will you punish me?"

I shake my head. "No more questions. Do you want to try it or not?" I can feel my patience wearing thin, which is going to make the entire concept difficult. Daddy Doms take their time with their women and control their emotions all the time. It will be interesting to see how I get on with it if she agrees.

She nods. "Sure."

I smile at her agreement. It's crazy how happy it makes me that she agreed to try this out with me and give me that trust. "We'll need to pick a safe word."

"A safe word?"

I nod in response. "Yeah, it's a word for when we are getting intimate. If you want to stop, you shout it out."

Her brow furrows. "Can't I just say stop?"

I laugh. "That's not normally how it works, as you might want to incorporate non-consent into a scene, so stop doesn't work." I rub a hand across my chin. "I like to go with the classic red. I think it works well."

Scarlett nods. "Okay, red it is then."

I stand up, unbuckling my belt. "Now, it's time for daddy to take care of his little girl. Undress for me, Scarlett."

Her eyes dilate as she stands eagerly, pulling her dress over her head and leaving it in a pile on the floor.

"Don't put your clothes on the floor, darlin'. I want you to keep the room tidy. Do you understand?"

Her eyes widen slightly, and she nods. "Yes, daddy," she easily regresses into the innocent role. She picks the dress up off the floor and saunters toward the closet, glancing over her shoulder to see if I'm watching as she goes.

It's a teasing fucking move that makes me want to chase after her and fuck her in the closet, but I control myself.

When she returns, she's naked. Her nipples are hard peaks, and it makes my cock so hard it hurts. It's ridiculous how much I desire her after fucking her mere hours ago, before we went to dinner.

"Good girl, now lie down on the bed for me."

She gives me an innocent look. "What for, daddy?"

I groan, shaking my head. "Don't question me and do as you're told."

She pouts before walking past me and lying down on the bed. Her legs are pressed tightly together, hiding her perfect little pussy nestled between her thighs.

"Spread your legs for me."

Her pink cheeks darken as she slowly parts them, watching me intently.

I take in the sight of her like this, spread and ready for me. Scarlett is taking a chance and trusting me. A dangerous thing to do, but I hope I won't let her down.

Whether Scarlett can trust me with her emotions remains to be seen. I don't know myself. The only thing I do know is that Scarlett is important to me, and I'll do anything to keep her around.

I crawl toward her on the bed and part her legs further. "It's about time I taste my little girl, isn't it?" I ask, my eyes fixed on her perfect pussy.

Scarlett shivers as I grab hold of her thighs, parting them. Slowly, I lick her clit, making her moan in ecstasy.

My cock is harder than a rock in my boxer briefs, making it hard to think straight. Scarlett tastes amazing, and I'm sure I'll never get enough of her. "Does that feel good, darlin'?" I ask, gazing up at her.

She looks utterly perfect with flushed cheeks, and her red hair splayed over the pillow messily. "Yes, daddy. It feels really good."

I groan and bury my head between her thighs again, licking her deeper this time.

She bucks her hips upward, pressing herself harder into my face.

I grab hold of her hips gently, resisting the urge to be more forceful. "Don't move, baby girl."

She pouts. "Sorry."

It's crazy how well she falls into her role as a submissive. I feel this is something she needs to open up to me.

"Now hold still while I look after you."

Scarlett's chest heaves up and down as I move my tongue through her soaking wet center, teasing her. I keep my tongue working her clit and slide my fingers in and out of her, pushing her toward release. I have learned how to coax her orgasm quicker than anyone I've ever been with.

"Fuck, daddy," she cries as her orgasm overwhelms her. I watch as her body writhes in front of me and her pussy gushes all over the sheets.

I spank her thigh and meet her gaze. "No foul language. Don't make me wash your mouth out with soap." I hold her gaze. "Or better yet, my cum."

Scarlett's eyes light up, and it's at that moment I realize I haven't made her suck me even once yet.

I move my hand to my belt and unbuckle it. "Do you like sucking things, darlin'?"

Scarlett nods eagerly. "Yes, daddy. I love sucking things." She places a finger in her mouth and sucks, demonstrating that she loves it.

My cock leaks in my boxer briefs as I chuck my pants on the floor. I stand and walk to the side of the bed. "Daddy wants to give you something better than your finger to suck, baby girl."

I drag the fabric of my boxer briefs down my hips and free my hard, aching cock. Scarlett's eyes widen as she plays the innocent girl. "Am I supposed to suck that, daddy?" she asks, lying down on her front so she's facing me. "It's so big. Do you think it will fit in my mouth?"

I groan. "Yes, baby. I'm sure it will. Why don't you try?"

She places her hand around my shaft and tugs twice, making me leak everywhere. "Okay." Slowly, she closes her mouth around me, and it feels like pure heaven.

Her mouth bobs up and down on my shaft as she sucks. The desperate need to shove every inch into the back of her throat claws at me. I grab Scarlett's hair and yank her head back. "That feels fucking amazing," I growl, kissing her. "But I want to fuck your throat. Will you let me do that?"

She looks into my eyes, and I can tell she has some reservations about trusting me. "Yes," she murmurs.

I groan and keep hold of her hair as my need to dominate more roughly rises to the surface. It's hard to change my basal desires. "Open wide." She opens her mouth, and I slide my cock to the back of her throat, surprised when she doesn't gag.

I thrust in and out faster, and she still doesn't gag. She hardly seems fazed by the pounding of my cock against the back of her throat. It's the best feeling I've ever experienced.

"Fuck, baby girl. Do you have no gag reflex?" I ask, pulling my cock from her mouth.

She shrugs, staring up at me with those big blue eyes. "I don't know. I guess not."

I lean down and kiss her. "You are perfection." I feel a twinge in my chest as I say it, knowing that ever letting her go is going to be impossible.

"Are you going to come down my throat?" she asks, batting her eyelashes as if my dirty little girl doesn't know what she's doing to me by suggesting such a thing.

"Yes. I'm going to feed you my cum. Would you like that?"

She nods eagerly, and it's almost enough to unravel me.

"Keep your mouth open wide for me then, darlin'."

She opens her jaw wide on my command. I thrust my throbbing cock deep into her throat repeatedly, driving myself closer to release. Scarlett is my perfect little submissive slut, as she takes it so well.

"I'm going to come, baby," I growl, unleashing my thick cum down her throat.

Scarlett swallows, struggling to keep up as some of it lands on her tongue and drips out of her mouth. She looks amazing with my cum dripping from her chin.

Neither of us can shake this desire we have for each other. We're caught in each other's webs. I don't see myself ever tiring of Scarlett.

15

SCARLETT

I turn over in bed and glance at the man lying by my side.

To say I am confused would be an understatement. Whatever is happening between us is starting to get too personal. Last night I told him about my father, which makes him the second person on this planet who knows. His reaction scares me a little, and I can't stop replaying what he said over and over in my mind.

I'm going to make sure that man can't touch another child ever again.

I think I've underestimated what Malachy is capable of and how far his darkness goes. If he intends to kill my father, I wouldn't exactly have any complaints other than it being illegal. My father is the kind of man that doesn't deserve to be living, not after what he did to his child and countless others.

What confuses me more than anything is why I told

him the truth. I shouldn't trust Malachy, not after the way he so savagely took my virginity without hesitation. I asked him not to, but he did it anyway.

It should have made me distrust him, but he was right. I had no say in the matter after he paid me two and a half million dollars for my virginity. It belonged to him, and he was taking what he paid for.

I can't understand his change in heart, asking me if I want to be his little girl. I still don't entirely understand what it means. I'm not sure if I have a choice, as he's made it clear every step of how he is in charge.

Ever since he picked me up at that auction, we've had a raw, palpable connection. It's there no matter how much I try to ignore it. He has broken down my walls and sunk his claws right into my heart.

Malachy grumbles in his sleep, startling me.

I swing my legs over the edge of the bed, knowing the last thing I want is for him to catch me watching him sleep. He's so brutally handsome in a way I didn't think I'd be drawn to. I've never met a man I'm so sexually attracted to before.

I scrub my hands over my face before stretching my arms over my head. This situation is fucked up. My phone vibrates on the nightstand, and my stomach sinks when I see *Mom* on the front.

Grabbing it, I switch the vibrations off and let it go to voicemail. The last thing I'm going to do is talk to my mom while Malachy is in the room. We've been texting, but this is the first time she's tried to ring.

A voicemail pops through, and I get up and head into the bathroom to listen to it.

Hopefully, she's okay. I hate ignoring a call from her, especially while she is sick. I close the door behind me and lock it before listening to the voicemail.

"Hey sweetheart, it's mom. I wanted to check in with you, but I guess you're busy with work. Call me when you get a moment. Love you." The message ends, and I feel relieved it was just a catch-up call. I worry about her every day that I'm not there, wondering how she's coping.

A knock at the door makes me jump. "Is everything okay, darlin'?" Malachy asks.

I clear my throat. "Yes, just freshening up," I reply.

"Okay, don't take too long. I've got plans for us today."

I swallow hard and stare at myself in the mirror.

What the fuck am I doing?

Malachy is a criminal. He's a dangerous man, and I've agreed to play some fucked up role for him. A role that, for some weird reason, appeals to me. I've never felt more confused before in my entire life.

I turn on the faucet to the sink and lean over it, trying to gather my composure. I don't know what Malachy could have planned for us. It means that I won't get a chance today to call my mom.

I want to be alone when I speak to her. It's hard enough lying to her, let alone with Malachy breathing down my neck as I do. The cool water is soothing as I splash it over my face, letting it settle my anxiety.

When I'm ready, I return to the bedroom to find Malachy sitting on the edge of the bed in his boxer briefs. "What were you doing, baby girl?"

I shake my head. "I told you, freshening up."

He shakes his head. "No, don't lie to me. You don't need a phone to freshen up. Who were you contacting?"

My stomach twists. "I was listening to a message from my mom."

His eyes narrow. "Why did you lie to me the first two times I asked then?"

I shrug. "I was freshening up too. It wasn't a complete lie."

"Come here." He points at his knee. "Over my knee."

I stare at him for a few seconds, wondering if he's joking. Then our conversation from the day before comes to the forefront of my mind.

When you are a naughty girl and don't do as daddy says, I will have to punish you.

My heart rate speeds up and my stomach churns. "Are you serious?"

He smirks devilishly, looking more handsome than ever. "Did you forget the rules already, baby girl?" The smirk drops and his eyes turn hard. "Over my knee, now. Don't make me come over there."

I walk toward him and bend over his lap, feeling a

little odd. The weirdest thing about it is the way my pussy gets wet.

Why would I be excited about being punished?

The moment Malachy sets his large hands on my ass cheeks, parting them slightly, I can't help but moan.

I can feel the hard press of his throbbing cock against my tummy. I'm turned on by this position and the way he has me at his mercy, even if my mind recoils at submitting control.

Malachy brings one of his hands back and spanks my left ass cheek hard enough for it to sting. "Liars must be punished. I don't want you to lie to me again, do you understand?"

I bite my bottom lip. "Yes, daddy. I'm sorry," I reply.

He spanks my right cheek a little harder. "Good girl." He caresses the stinging skin of my ass cheeks. "But I'm not sure you've learned your lesson yet." He spanks me again, even harder and with faster succession between each slap of skin against skin.

I writhe over his lap, feeling the need increase between my thighs. "Fuck, Malachy," I cry, wanting nothing more than to feel every inch of his huge, thick cock stretching me.

This man has converted me into a horny creature that can't get enough. I wonder whether it would have been different with someone else. The pure attraction I felt when our eyes first met tells me it couldn't have been the same with any other man.

THE TOWN CAR comes to a stop, and I gaze out of the window.

We left the city a little while back and have been driving for about thirty minutes. Malachy has been quiet for the ride, working on his laptop. He still hasn't looked up as we pull into a parking lot.

"Where are we?" I ask.

Malachy finally looks up from the screen. "Are you telling me you live in Boston and have never been out here?" I nod, brow furrowed. "Yeah, pretty sure I don't know where we are."

"We're at Walden Pond. It's a nice nature reservation with a little beach on the pond's edge." He shrugs. "I thought it would be a nice place to explore and relax together."

The sentiment confuses me as I question what is happening between us.

Is this a business transaction or something more?

"Sounds nice," I say, returning my attention out of the window as the driver parks the car.

Malachy gets out first, and the driver opens my door. He reaches to help me out, but Malachy shoves him out of the way. "Let me." He glares at the driver with possessiveness.

"Sir," he says, bowing his head slightly and backing away.

"Come on, darlin'. We can relax on the beach first."

He grabs my hand and glances at the driver. "Can you bring the loungers, please?"

He nods. "Of course, sir."

I watch as the driver pulls two foldable loungers out of the trunk and carries them both behind us as we head toward a large, gleaming lake. "It's very picturesque here," I say, feeling calm being surrounded by nature. As a little kid, I always loved the woods and being outdoors. City life can be a drag, but I always headed out to Cape Cod or something. I never knew this was on my doorstep.

"It's quiet today. It can get pretty busy if you come at the wrong time." Malachy leads me toward the water's edge and grabs one lounger off his driver.

He sets one lounger down before yanking the other from him. "That's all thanks, Mick. I'll let you know when we're ready to leave."

He nods. "Sir." I watch as he walks away from us.

"How come you talk to your staff that way?" I ask, wondering why he was rude to his driver, making him carry the loungers down to the beach.

Malachy narrows his eyes. "What way?"

I shrug. "You were pretty rude."

He growls. "Are you questioning how I speak to my staff, Scarlett?"

I bite my lip, knowing that warning tone. "No, I was just asking—"

He yanks me against him and grabs my ass cheeks

in both of his hands. "Don't tempt me to punish you here; we're not exactly alone, darlin'."

I swallow hard. We're far from alone. There are at least twenty other people scattered over the beach.

"Sorry, daddy," I whisper, worried someone might hear as the nearest couple are about ten feet from us.

He kisses me passionately before murmuring against my lips. "Good girl, I want you to be good and do as I say for the rest of the day, or else I won't hesitate to spank you right here in front of everyone."

A shudder pulses through me at the thought of being so publicly humiliated.

"Yes, daddy," I say against his lips, feeling my nipples tighten against the thin fabric of my dress. "Are we going for a swim?" I ask, glancing at the gleaming water in front of us.

"Sure, I have a bikini for you if you want to change up in the woods." He holds out a few strands of fabric, which will hardly cover me up. Not something I'd normally choose to wear, but it's my only choice.

"Okay, I'll be back in a minute." I take the bikini and head toward the cover of trees at the back of the beach.

I hide behind a large tree and strip my clothes off, quickly changing into the bikini, which is beyond revealing. It barely covers my breasts, and the bottoms are like a thong.

Malachy is relaxing, lying on a lounger with his

hands behind his head. He looks at peace at the side of the lake.

I return to him and sit down on the other lounger.

He whistles when he sees me in the bikini. "Smoking hot, baby girl."

I shake my head. "Don't be silly."

He sits up and removes his sunglasses. "I'm not being silly, it's the truth. You're hotter than fire." His brow raises. "How about we go for a dip to cool off?" There's a devilish glint in his eyes which tells me his mind has gone straight to the gutter.

I shrug. "It is hot, and I wouldn't mind a dip."

He smiles and stands, holding out his hand to me. "Come on then, darlin'."

I take it and allow him to pull me to my feet, following him to the water's edge. The tepid water laps over my feet as we walk in. Malachy pulls me quickly into the deepening water, not giving me a chance to get used to the temperature change.

"Ah, it's cold," I complain, trying to pull my hand from his grasp. "At least give me a chance to get used to it."

He tugs me right up to my neck in water and laughs. "No, it's best to get it over and done with, like ripping off a Band-Aid."

I shake my head. Malachy wraps his arms around me, pulling me close. "I'm not sure I agree."

He presses his lips to mine. "I'm not sure it matters, baby girl. Remember who is in charge."

I nod and pout slightly, trying to fit into my role. "Sorry, daddy."

He groans, forcing me to turn around and molding himself against me.

I feel the hot press of his cock against my ass cheeks, making me wet between my thighs. When I'm with Malachy, it's a permanent problem, always turned on whenever his hands are on me.

"You are a filthy little girl, aren't you, Scarlett?" he purrs into my ear, making the hair on the back of my neck stand on end.

"Yes, your filthy girl, daddy."

He bites my shoulder hard enough to hurt, making my nipples tighten against the skimpy fabric of the bikini. "I love how filthy you are." He suddenly slips a finger inside of me, moving aside the fabric of the bikini bottoms.

"Malachy," I gasp, shocked that he'd do this in such a public place. "What are you doing?"

He bites my shoulder again, harder this time. "No questions."

I groan, focusing my attention on not crying out as he plunges his finger in and out of me, hard and fast. He keeps going until I'm so desperate for his cock that I'm panting.

"Please, daddy," I whine quietly.

He nips at my earlobe. "Please, what?"

I bite my lip, trying to stop myself from saying it out loud. It's no use. I need to feel Malachy inside of me, no matter who sees us. "Fuck me," I whisper. He chuckles. "So naughty. What about all these people here?" He pulls his finger out of me, making me whimper at the emptiness. Slowly, he turns me around so I'm facing him. "Do you think you can take my cock without crying out, baby girl?"

I honestly don't know if I can keep quiet, but right now, I don't care. "Who cares? I need you now," I whine, clinging onto Malachy's broad shoulders as he holds me in the water.

"Careful what you wish for." He positions me over his cock and slams me down over it, making me cry out.

Quickly, he presses his lips to mine to drown out the scream. His tongue delves into my mouth as he slowly thrusts his hips, fucking me with deep, slow strokes. Hopefully, onlookers would assume we're a loved-up couple making out in the lake, not fucking beneath the water.

I moan softly against his lips. "Fuck, yes, daddy," I whisper.

He smiles against my lips. "Such a dirty mouth, baby girl. I'll have to wash it out with cum when we get home and give you a good spanking."

I moan at the thought, feeling my thighs quiver and my release creep nearer. "I can't believe we're fucking in public." Just over a week ago, I was a virgin who had never had sex. Now, I'm fucking at a public lake with at least twenty people nearby. Thankfully, all of them are adults. It's insane the way Malachy has changed me into a dirty girl who can't get enough.

"It's the best way to fuck. The risk of getting caught makes it that much hotter." He bites my bottom lip. "A couple of dirty fuckers know and are stroking their cocks and watching."

My stomach churns, but my pussy gets wetter at the thought of other people getting off by watching us. "Are you serious?"

Malachy laughs. "Very." He turns me around to see, and I notice two young guys watching at the back of the beach, their cocks in their hands as they stroke themselves. Neither seems to care that they are in full view of everyone.

"They are crazy."

Malachy turns me back around. "Dirty fuckers. If they ever tried to touch you, I'd kill them," he growls. "Now, I only want you to look at one cock, and that's mine. Do you understand?"

I nod. "Yes, daddy."

"Good girl," he murmurs, before kissing me again.

He fucks me harder and faster, as if forgetting to hide what we're doing.

I can feel myself getting closer and closer to release with each thrust. Malachy is right. It's the hottest sex we've had yet, all because we're in public. "I'm going to come," I warn him, clawing my fingernails into his shoulders to stop myself from crying out too loud.

"Come on daddy's cock in front of all these people," he growls into my ear like an animal.

"Oh, my—"

Malachy kisses me, swallowing my cries of pleasure as I come all over his cock. He grunts against my lips, releasing all of his cum deep inside of me. Even as I come down from the orgasm, he's still thrusting in and out, making sure every drop is drained.

Once finished, he pulls out of me and fixes my bikini bottoms back in place. We swim around for a short while before making our way back to the loungers. I notice the guys no longer have their cocks out on the beach and keep their gazes off us as we leave the water.

We push our loungers together and lazily hold each other's hands. There's a genuine smile on Malachy's face that makes him more handsome.

There's a change in him here, relaxing on a lounger on the beach. It's nice to see this side of him—a side not ruled by danger and darkness. We both drift off for a short while until his cell phone rings.

He glances at it before tossing it back down on the lounger. I smile, as it's the first time since I met him I've seen him ignore a call.

Suddenly, the phone rings again, and Malachy's easy demeanor fades. "Son of a bitch." He picks up the call. "What the fuck do you—" He stops mid-sentence, and that's when I hear someone calling Malachy's name.

My heart skips a beat as I see Mick running toward us.

"On my way," Malachy says, canceling the call.

"What has happened?" I ask.

He shakes his head. "No time to explain. There's an emergency, and I need to get back." He grabs my hand. "Come on, baby girl. We're going to cut our day trip short."

Mick doesn't need to be asked as he grabs the two loungers and heads back to the parking lot behind us.

Once we're in the car, there's silence between us until we reach the city limits. Malachy turns toward me.

"You're not safe with me right now, Scarlett." His jaw ticks. "Where can I take you that is safe?"

My heart skips a beat, and I wonder if he's going to let me go to my mom's. "I'd like to go home with my mom."

There's a flash of hurt in his eyes, but he nods. "Okay. What's the address?"

I tell the driver the address and sit back in my seat. There's a weird sinking feeling in my gut as we drive back to my home. The atmosphere between us is tense and silent.

All this time I've wanted to know when I'd go back home. I'm getting my wish, but I'm torn about it. All I want is to stay right here with Malachy.

16

MALACHY

Scarlett reaches for the door handle, but I jerk her away from it. "Remember, Scarlett. This is a temporary setback. You'll return to me in a couple of days once the heat has died down."

She looks me in the eye, and I can see the happiness in them ever since I told her she could go back to her mom's. I haven't seen her that happy since I met her. "Of course, no problem."

Scarlett tries to move again, but I can't let her go that easily.

"Where's my goodbye kiss, baby girl?"

Her cheeks stain a deep pink as she leans toward me and presses her lips tentatively to mine. I pull her close and deepen the kiss, knowing that no amount of time with her in my arms will be enough.

Once I finally allow her to break away, we're both

panting for air. "I'll miss doing that for the next couple of days."

She nods. "Me too."

There's a palpable need in the air sparking between us. A need that makes me want to tell Mick to take a hike while I fuck her right here in the back of the car in broad daylight. I keep control and let her hand go. "I'll be in touch when you can return to me."

She nods and reaches for the door. This time I allow her to get out and leave. It hurts me more than I explain to watch her walk into that apartment block and away from me, even if it's temporary.

There's an unspoken question lying between us that clouds our every moment together in tension.

When will I let her go permanently?

Officially, I've already taken what I paid for before I intended to. Scarlett could demand that I release her since I've taken her virginity, but she hasn't. Although there was nothing official about the illegal auction we took part in.

A part of me never wants to let her go. I can't believe my second-in-command got caught up in a botched attempt to cut off Milo's laundering operations. Mazzeo knew where we were going to be and when. It means there's a mole in our clan. A mole that I need to weed out fast.

Niall will live, according to Seamus, but he's sustained severe injuries, which will put him out of work for a month at least. I need him now more than ever, which means I need to look at my guys and work out who I can trust. Seamus is a decent guy and loyal, but I can't trust him to step into Niall's shoes. He doesn't have the intelligence to help me run things.

Aiden is my next best guy after Niall. He's been in the clan for almost as long as Niall. I'm certain he wouldn't betray me. It has to be one of the lower-level clan members. The journey from central Boston to my home in Beacon Hills is longer than normal because the traffic is hectic. Trust the traffic to be like this when there's a fucking emergency I need to deal with.

The basement of my home is a makeshift hospital, and the doctor is already patching up Niall. He should be out of surgery soon.

Milo's guys shot him three times when they ambushed them, trying to set up explosives at his club. Men were waiting at all of his establishments, ready to stop our plan before it started.

Mick pulls through the gates and parks in front of my home.

I get out and march into my house, cracking my neck as tension builds. Niall is like a brother to me, and I will make Milo pay for shooting my lad. It seems he wanted payback for me shooting his capo, Piero.

The son of a bitch lived, so I don't get what the big deal is.

Aiden is standing at the entrance to the basement and straightens up when he sees me. "Sir, you are here."

He clears his throat. "Niall is just out of surgery, and the surgeon is certain he will make it."

Relief washes through me. Although the doctor had said he'd live, there's always a risk when going under the knife. "Good. What other casualties did we have?"

Seamus appears from behind me. "Three dead, five injured in total, boss."

I turn to face him. "Who died?"

"Patrick, Conor, and unfortunately, Oisin, your cousin, sir." I feel the rage tightening inside of me. Milo hasn't killed one of my cousins but two. My uncle will be beside himself. "Does Dara know yet?"

Seamus shakes his head. "No, we thought you might want to break the news to him since he's your uncle."

Fucking cowards are too scared of my uncle, which is hilarious. The guy is a waste of space and always has been. If there is anyone they should be scared of, it's me. I built this bloody clan with my bare hands.

"Might be best coming from family after Sean's death." I shake my head. "The guy won't take it well."

Seamus nods. "Aye, that's what we thought."

I turn my back on him and head down into the basement of my home. Some people have home cinemas or saunas, but I've got a fucking fully fledged hospital with all the latest gear. We must keep work-related injuries out of the public hospitals. Otherwise, we'd have the police breathing down our necks.

I see Niall lying unconscious on the first bed, but

I'm surprised when I see Alicia sitting next to him holding his hand.

My brow furrows as I watch her, noticing the tear-stained cheeks. Alicia knows Niall and has done since we were kids. I didn't think they were very close.

"Sis, what are you doing down here?" My voice startles her as she drops Niall's hand and stands.

"I heard what happened and wanted to see if I could help at all." She shakes her head, glancing back at Niall. "I can't believe Niall got caught up in this. Why did you send your best man to do such a dangerous job?"

I grit my teeth, feeling irritated at being questioned by my baby sister. "I left him in charge of cutting the fucking Italians off by shutting down their laundering operations across the city." I shake my head, glancing at Niall. "He came up with the idea and organized it. I didn't tell him to be on the front line, for fuck's sake."

Alicia cries, and I wonder why she's so twisted up about this.

"What is it to you, anyway? You knew Niall when we were kids, but I didn't think you kept in touch."

Her brow furrows. "Of course we do. Niall's in this house as much as you are, if not more."

I shake my head and walk to the other side of Niall's bed, looking down at my man, who looks utterly broken. "Whoever did this, I'll fucking kill them, Niall." I place a gentle hand on his shoulder. "Someone betrayed us to the Italians, and they will pay."

Alicia stands opposite me. "Is violence always your answer, Brother?"

I meet her gaze. "It's a stupid question, Alicia."

She sits down in the chair next to Niall's bed. "Why was Niall in charge of this? Where were you?"

Guilt claws at me as I was relaxing with a girl that I can't seem to get out of my brain—a girl that has turned me soft. "I was taking a day off."

Alicia's eyes narrow. "With the virgin that you bought at the auction?"

"Yeah, what of it?"

"There's something different about this one, isn't there?" She shakes her head. "I mean, when I saw her contentedly walking the grounds without a scratch or bruise on her, I knew there had to be."

I glare at Alicia, hoping she will get the message to leave it alone. "I don't know what you're talking about."

She laughs. "I hope she will finally be the end of your sick and twisted obsession with those auctions. She seems like a nice girl."

I growl at my sister. "Yes, a girl you told my life fucking story to."

Alicia holds her hands up. "We merely had a conversation. Girl to girl."

"Well, don't in the future. I don't want you talking to Scarlett, do you understand?"

She raises a brow. "Wow, you have it bad for her, Mal."

I hate it when my sister calls me Mal. She does it to

wind me up, so I've stopped reacting. "Whatever," I grunt, turning my attention to the other four beds occupied by my injured men.

Two of them I don't recognize. The other two are Oscar and Rory. Two men have been with us for a while but are nothing more than soldiers in my clan. "Who are the other two guys here?" I ask Seamus, looking over at their beds.

Seamus' brow furrows. "Brian and Craig Samson, brothers that have been with the clan for three years."

I run a hand across the back of my neck. "Shit, I need to keep a better tab on who we let into the clan. I don't think I've met them, for fuck's sake."

Seamus nods. "Maybe we haven't been selective enough of who we let into the clan. Someone has betrayed us, and we need to find out who."

Aiden approaches. "Do you want me to arrange a sit down with the entire clan?"

I nod. "Sure, lad, make it for tomorrow. We can't delay finding the rat as fast as possible. If I have to lock the entire clan in a room for questioning tomorrow to root him out, I will."

Aiden nods. "Sure, I'll text you the location tonight." He pats Seamus on the shoulder. "See you tomorrow."

Seamus nods. "Sure, lad."

I watch as Aiden walks out of the basement, falling into Niall's place as naturally as if he had always been doing it. Seamus looks a little irritated that he got passed up for the job, but I don't care. Aiden is more trustworthy. "I'll need both you guys to work together and help our while Niall's not about."

Seamus nods. "Anything you need, boss."

I glance over at Alistair, our resident surgeon. "Alistair, do you need help tonight?"

He looks up and nods. "Yes, I can't deal with five by myself. If you can send a couple of guys to give me a hand, that would be grand."

I nod and glance at Seamus. "Can you arrange that for me, lad?"

"Sure, I'll get onto it now." I watch as Seamus walks away, leaving me, Alicia, and Alistair. Alicia is back by Niall's side. "I'll help here tonight. It's the least I can do."

Alistair smiles. "That would be great, Alicia, since you're a trained nurse."

She nods. "Yes, makes sense for me to help instead of some knuckleheads that don't know what they're doing."

I narrow my eyes. "Fine, but don't be overworking yourself, Sis." I turn to leave the basement. "I'll see you all tomorrow." I walk away, wondering why my sister is so obsessed suddenly with Niall's welfare.

I sit at the head of the table, staring at all the men in my clan.

My first night without Scarlett by my side was rough. I hardly got any sleep, and it doesn't help that I've been worrying about Niall. It was necessary to get her away from my house while the threat is so close to home. A rat in our ranks spells danger.

Out of all the men, I probably only know half of their names. It's bad that I've allowed the recruitment of new members to get a little out of hand. It would have been easy for Milo to pay a traitorous Irish lad to apply and join our ranks, feeding information to him.

The only thing worse than a snitch is a snitch that rats out his kind. I clear my throat. "We have a rat in our ranks." A low whispering breaks out among the guys.

I clap my hands. "Silence, lads." I shake my head. "We ain't leaving this room until I've rooted him out by whatever fucking means necessary."

"How do ya know there's a rat?" A young lad shouts out.

I roll my eyes. "It's not important how I know. Someone ratted us out to the Italians. They couldn't have known our plan without it being leaked, so if the rat wants to make this as painless as possible, he'll reveal his cowardly ass now."

I notice movement to the back of the room, and suddenly a guy I don't recognize makes a run for the door. He makes it, but the door is locked.

"Well done. That was easy." I stand and approach the young man who stares at me with such fear it makes the dark side of me rejoice. "You're the little bastard who got Niall shot."

He shakes his head. "I didn't mean to. Milo has my kid, and I had to do what he says." He's shaking in his boots.

"That's a fucking lie, lad." I grab hold of his shoulder and push him hard against the door. "I doubt you've even got a kid at your age, and one thing Milo never does is fuck with children."

I slam my fist hard into his nose, breaking it immediately.

He groans as I punch him hard in the gut, feeling my rage take over. This fucking bastard almost killed my best friend. He killed three of my guys, including my cousin, even if it was indirect.

"You are the reason my cousin is dead," I growl, letting go of his collar and allowing him to slump to the floor in a heap. I kick him hard in the face, breaking his jaw. As always, my enemies always pay the price. I have no limits to my violence when it comes to the people that cross me.

"I'm going to kill you with my bare fucking hands, and I want this to be a lesson to the rest of you." I turn around, glancing at the mix of shocked expressions and blank ones. The men that know me the best expect this. "Anyone that crosses me dies."

I grab hold of the pathetic waste of space and tighten my hands around his throat. His eyes widen as he tries to breathe, struggling as I cut off his airways.

Many leaders would leave the dirty work to their men, but I'm not like others. I came from the bottom up, and I'm not afraid to get my hands dirty.

The struggling sounds of the man who is nearing death punctuates the silence in the room.

I look into his eyes, feeling nothing at all as I watch the life drain from them. He is the reason three other men are dead, so it's only right he dies too. An eye for an eye is the fairest concept in my book.

His life leaves him, and I stand up. My knuckles are bloody from punching him, and I pull a handkerchief out of my pocket to wipe them off. The silence is poignant.

I nod to the guy standing by the door. He and another guy come forward and drag the traitor's body out of the room.

I return to my chair. "Now, does anyone else want to betray me to my enemies?" I ask, glancing around the room.

A lot of the men stare back at me with fear. I'm used to it, but the men I know are most loyal stare back at me with unwavering confidence. They know they'd never be in that position because they'd die before they betrayed the McCarthy clan.

I clap my hands. "Good." I run a hand across the back of my neck and glance to my right at Aiden. "Can you brief the men on the current situation with the war against the Italians?"

Aiden nods. "Aye, sir." He stands. "The Italians

thwarted our plan to cut off their laundering operations, which means it's no longer a viable option." He
glances at me briefly. "That means we need to work out
a way to cut them off before they make it to the city
limits. It's going to take a tremendous team effort to
surveil their routes and learn them before trying to
strike."

Seamus stands. "Yeah, we only get one shot at it,
and we can't fuck it up this time."

I watch the men who belong to my clan, making a
note of who I know and don't. "Also, I want all of you
to report to me after this meeting ends if I don't know
you by name." I run a hand over my beard. "It's about
time I knew everyone's name in this clan. We are going
to tighten criteria for getting in here since that dead
bastard whose name I don't even fucking know was a
snitch."

A few faces pale.

Who can blame them after what they witnessed me do?

My darkness knows no bounds, and my violence has
no limits. They knew what they were signing up for
when they joined the clan. I'll never apologize for who
I am.

17

SCARLETT

I stare at my phone, willing it to ring. It's been one week since Malachy dropped me off here without so much as an explanation, other than being around him was too dangerous.

What the fuck is that supposed to mean?

He said he'd call me in a couple of days. I don't even have his cell phone number, so I can't contact him until he calls. It's driving me crazier than I ever expected. All the time, I'd been wondering when he'd let me go home. Now that he has, I can't wait to be back in his bed. It's pathetic.

My mom bought my story that the production had to be rescheduled and that they'd call me back once they needed me. Although, as time goes on, she seems to ask more and more questions—questions I don't have the answer to.

It feels like I'm slowly digging myself into a bigger hole with every lie I tell.

"Morning, sweetheart," my mom says, poking her head through the crack in the door. "It's ten o'clock, don't you want some breakfast?"

I shake my head. "I'm not hungry. What time is your hospital appointment today?"

"It's at one-thirty this afternoon. You don't have to come, Scarlett. I can go by myself."

"No chance. I haven't been able to be at the other appointments, but I'm not missing this one."

My mom smiles. "Well, the doctors are positive that they can get me into remission in no time."

I sigh a breath of relief, but I want to hear it from the doctor's mouth today. Once I do, I'll feel easier about it all. The thought of losing the one person I care about in this world scares the living daylights out of me.

My feelings for Malachy are confusing.

Could I care about him too?

It seems ridiculous that I could have feelings for a man who practically bought me for sex. Romantic feelings and being bought don't exactly go hand in hand, yet I long for him.

Whatever we had together, it wasn't just sex. It was deeper and profound. A connection that went beyond physical attraction that I can't quite explain.

"I'm so glad, Mom. I don't know what I'd do without you." I feel my throat closing up at the thought of losing her.

My mom walks in, tears in her eyes, and sits down next to me. I lean against her, allowing her to hold me. "You would be fine, sweetheart, as I've raised a strong woman." She kisses my cheek. "But I'm not going anywhere. Not yet, anyway." She smiles. "I hope to be around long enough to see you walk down the aisle and have children of your own someday."

My heart skips a beat that the moment she mentions walking down the aisle, Malachy's face pops into my head. A stupid notion since he's about as far from marriage material as you can get.

"I'm not sure that will happen soon, if ever."

My mom laughs. "Don't be silly, Scarlett. You are young and have plenty of time to find the right man if that's what you want."

I can't understand why part of me wants that, but with Malachy. A man that could never provide a stable home for me, let alone children.

I shrug. "We'll see. Has Frank been over a lot while I was gone?"

My mom blushes instantly at the mention of our next-door neighbor. "Oh yes, lovely man. He's helped quite a lot."

I raise a brow. "Why are you blushing?"

She clears her throat. "I don't know what you're talking about."

"Did something happen between you and Frank?" I ask, as I've had a hunch about him ever since he moved in next door. He's had his eye on my mom, but he seems like a good guy. Mom hasn't considered dating ever since my dad was imprisoned. I think his disgusting treatment of me made it hard for her to trust men, as well.

"Now, I don't want you to jump to conclusions, but Frank and I have been on a couple of dates." She shrugs. "After you mentioned he had the hots for me, I flirted a little to see if you were right." She laughs. "Turns out he's wanted to ask me out ever since he moved in, but it's nothing serious."

I smile. "Well, as long as Frank treats you well, that's all I care about."

My cell phone rings, and both me and my mom look at it. The number is blocked, and I instantly believe it has to be Malachy.

"Oh, I wonder if that's the production calling you back?" She stands. "Take the call, and I'll make us some pancakes. I know you said you're not hungry, but you need to eat."

I nod and grab the phone, waiting until she shuts the door to accept the call. "Hello?"

"That took longer than is acceptable to answer, darlin'." Malachy drawls on the other end of the line, making my stomach flutter at the sound of his deep, rough voice. It's been too long since I last heard it.

"Sorry, I was speaking with my mom." I clear my throat. "I had expected to hear from you sooner."

There's a few moments of silence before Malachy chuckles. "Did you miss me that much, baby girl?"

I swallow hard, realizing that I shouldn't want him to call at all. "No, I expected to hear from you after a couple of days."

He clicks his tongue. "What has daddy told you? No lying."

My face heats. "It's true. Is it time for me to come back?" I ask, hoping my mom isn't listening on the other side of the door. She is nosy, so I need to keep what I say as basic as possible.

Malachy growls. "I'll punish you for lying to me, but unfortunately, no. I've got to attend to some business out of town. I'll be back in a week and will pick you up at your house a week from today."

My stomach sinks, hearing him tell me he's not coming for me yet. I swallow the lump that has formed in my throat. "What kind of business?" I ask.

"None you need to concern yourself with. I'll see you soon, darlin'." He cancels the call, making my chest ache.

It's clear that my obsession with Malachy is one-sided. He doesn't seem at all affected by our time apart, making me wonder if I've imagined his feelings for me the entire time.

I guess I have to wait another week to find out. I stand up and head out of my room toward the kitchen. My stomach sinks as I realize I've got another week of lying to my mom and digging myself a bigger hole.

"Was it the production company?"

I nod. "Yes, one more week of delays. They will

send someone to get me a week from today." I sink onto a stool opposite the hob on the island, resting my head in my hands. "At least I can spend one more week with you, Mom."

She smiles. "Yes, although I have got a weekend away planned with Frank. Only Saturday morning and back Monday morning. You'll be alright on your own, though, won't you?"

My eyes widen. "Wow, you said you'd been on a few dates. Isn't it too soon for a romantic weekend?"

She shakes her head. "I don't think so. When you know it's right, you know."

I sigh heavily, wishing that I didn't know it was right with a fucking criminal mastermind. Malachy is right for me, even if everything about his lifestyle is wrong.

My mom left with Frank early this morning, leaving me alone for the weekend.

We've spent the last four days together doing things we enjoy, and it's helped keep my mind off Malachy.

I can't deny that I'm going out of my mind not seeing or speaking to him. He has got under my skin with his treatment of me. The last time we were together, it felt like we were almost a couple. To have that ripped away so suddenly hurt in ways that I can't explain.

I look at my phone, and my heart skips a beat when

I notice the date. It's the sixth of July, which means I'm eight days late. My stomach churns, and my body trembles.

Fuck.

Malachy never mentioned using protection the entire time, and it never even entered my mind.

How could I be so stupid?

He probably thinks I'm on the pill or something. I hold my head in my hands, wondering if I could be pregnant with a mobster's baby. It's almost been three weeks since he 'fucked me in his woods and took my virginity.

At least Mom is away, so I can go to the drugstore and get a test. Hopefully, it's a coincidence, and I'm a little late.

Someone knocks at the apartment door, making me jump. I get up and answer it to find Kaia glaring at me. "Where the fuck have you been?"

Oh shit.

I had hoped to avoid Kaia. I haven't replied to her texts or calls, knowing that she would call me out on my lies. My mom is gullible. Kaia isn't.

"What do you mean?" I ask, trying to play dumb and give myself enough time to think of an excuse.

"You haven't replied to my texts or calls." She shakes her head. "You didn't turn up at work, so I came to see your mom about two weeks ago, and she told me about Broadway." Her eyes narrow. "It's a fucking lie, and you know it."

I swallow hard, opening the door to her. "Come in, and I'll explain."

She is pissed—more pissed than I've ever seen her. Kaia marches past me and sits down on the sofa, arms crossed over her chest. "I'm supposed to be your best friend, and you blank me like that. What the fuck, Scarlett?"

I sigh heavily, knowing she will give me a serious telling off for being so damn stupid. "I knew you wouldn't agree with what I've done."

Kaia sits straighter. "What have you done? Sold your kidney on the black market?"

I shake my head. "No, I sold my virginity at auction."

Kaia blinks a few times, looking at me blankly. "That's a thing?"

I nod. "Yeah, but it turns out it wasn't as simple as one night, and then I'm free." I swallow hard, thinking about the man who purchased it. Maybe there's something wrong with me for wanting more with Malachy, especially considering how we met.

"What the fuck were you thinking?"

I shrug. "I was desperate. We couldn't pay the debt to the loan shark, and there was no way we could afford the rest of my mom's treatment."

Kaia's expression softens. "Why didn't you come to me? You know I've got money stashed aside." Kaia's family is well off, but I would not beg my friend. It was more than she'd have stashed aside, anyway. There was no way I could ever repay her for the cash we needed.

I shake my head. "Because it would take my whole damn life to pay you back for the amount we needed, and I'm not sure you would have had enough." I sigh. "Anyway, the man that bought my virginity expects me to be his for up to a couple of months."

Her brow furrows. "So, why are you here?"

"He had to leave town for a couple of weeks. He'll be picking me up again on Monday." My stomach churns at the thought of seeing him again.

Kaia shakes her head. "Is he some gross old guy?"

"No, but he's a dangerous man." I run a hand through my hair nervously. "He's probably in his early thirties if I was to guess and the leader of a criminal organization."

"Fuck, what have you done, Scarlett?"

She doesn't know half of it. If I'm pregnant, then this situation just got a lot worse.

Kaia sits back. "At least you've finally lost your virginity. I thought you never would. How much did he pay?"

"You won't believe it." I twist my fingers together nervously. "Two and a half million dollars."

Kaia sits up. "No fucking way. You have the money?"

I nod. "Yes, minus the auctioneer's commission, which was twenty percent."

"Holy shit. That's insane." She narrows her eyes at me. "I hope you guys were safe, though."

I feel heat filtering to my face as I realize how stupid I've been. "No, in fact, I'm about eight days late."

Kaia holds a hand to her face. "Oh, Scarlett. Are you telling me you might be carrying a mobster's baby right now?"

I nod in response. "Possibly. I was about to go to the drugstore to get a test."

Kaia stands. "Okay, I'm coming with you. You need moral support for this."

I smile. "You don't have to... I've been a real ass keeping this from you." Guilt twists my gut as it's not only Kaia I've kept this from.

She nods. "Yeah, you have, but I get why you did." She laughs. "If you had told me about it beforehand, I definitely would have stopped you." Kaia holds her hand out to me, and I take it. "Now, let's find out the truth."

I nod in response, and we head out of the apartment to the drugstore on the corner. It's only a five-minute walk. My heart is pounding so hard I think I might pass out.

Kaia even pays for it to save me from embarrassment, since everyone knows my mom and me in this neighborhood.

I feel a bit of the weight lifted from my shoulders now that she knows. Or at least, some of it. The one thing I haven't told her is that since I met Malachy, I've developed feelings for him.

I know Kaia wouldn't approve, but I'll get to that bridge when I come to it.

We walk in a tense silence back to the apartment, both of us apprehensive about the results of the test I'm yet to take.

There's no way I'm cut out to be a mom, and I can say with pretty certain confidence that Malachy isn't father material either. We're both damaged in our own ways.

When we get to the apartment, Kaia shakes her head. "What are you going to do if it's positive?"

"I've not thought that far ahead yet." That at least is the truth.

"Okay, shall we get this over with?" Kaia crosses her fingers. "I'm praying it's going to be negative, Scarlett."

I swallow hard and nod, taking the test out of the bag. "I'll be right back." I walk into the bathroom and unpackage the test before peeing on the stick. It's gross as I put the cap back on and stare at the little digital screen, waiting to see my result.

Sixty seconds have never felt so long. When I see the cross appear, my heart sinks.

Pregnant.

I stare at the test for so long I don't know how long I've been in here, when Kaia bangs on the door. "Scarlett. Is everything alright?"

"Not really," I grumble.

She opens the door and takes one look at my face. "Fuck. It's positive. Isn't it?"

I nod, feeling the crushing weight of so many emotions overwhelm me. Tears fill my eyes.

She rushes over and pulls me into a tight hug. "Don't worry. Everything is going to be okay. We will work this out."

I feel tears streaming down my cheeks as I hold on to my friend, thankful she came over. Learning the news without her here would have made it much harder. I've got three days until Malachy comes to collect me—three days to work this out.

18

MALACHY

I've been stuck in Salem for six bloody days now.

The Italians are making it harder than we expected, but we're close to hitting them, though.

Every lorry load of drugs they take out of port, they switch the lorry at least three times along the way, taking the stash out of the way of Boston before returning. It's clever, but we've got all the time in the damn world.

Although, that's not entirely true. The longer this takes, the longer I'm held away from Scarlett. She is all I can think of most of the time, which is irritating.

I'm trying to fight a war, and all I can think about is a fucking woman.

I've typed out texts to her, only to delete them. If I let her know I'm thinking of her all the time, it will make this real.

I hate that we started exploring a new dynamic with each other, only to be forced to part from her the next day.

"Boss, we want to hit them this afternoon. What do you think?" Aiden asks, looking at me.

I've been zoned out of this meeting the entire time. Seamus, Cormac, and Brandon are staring at me expectantly.

"If you think it's best." They look a little surprised by my lack of input, as normally I run things.

Brandon nods. "We all agree. Let's hit them and get back to Boston."

"Yeah, the longer we hang around Salem, the most likely the Italians will work out what we're up to," Cormac says.

I crack my neck. "I should have killed Milo Mazzeo when I had the chance."

Aiden clears his throat. "Not sure that would have been wise, sir. You know Milo is vital in keeping stability in the city."

He reminds me so much of Niall, always my voice of reason, calming my rage and making me see the bigger picture. I clap him on the shoulder. "You're right, lad. I hate the fucking Italians."

Seamus laughs. "You ain't the only one."

"When do you guys want to strike? We're expecting a shipment tonight, but we can't strike the docks because it's Russian-owned territory."

Aiden nods. "Yeah, we can't do anything in Salem,

but we can follow the truck out of the city limits." Aiden shrugs. "Then, we hit them hard."

Cormac clears his throat. "Word around town is this is their largest shipment since they started running through Salem port. Two shipping containers, which means two lorries to take out."

"How many men are we getting to take them down? I don't want a fuck up like last time."

Seamus shakes his head. "There won't be, boss. We're getting eight guys on each truck. They may have a few guys on board, but not enough to overpower a surprise attack."

I hope he's right. The last thing we need right now is another mistake. The Italians are ahead of the game. Also, the word is Milo is going to be appointed to the city council any day now. It's going to make things difficult as he can hit us politically.

We need to step up our game, and this is the best place to start. Two shipping containers of cocaine isn't much to the Italians, but it will hurt his big ego.

"Who are you sending?" I ask.

Cormac clears his throat. "Aiden and I will take six of our best after one." He nods toward Seamus. "Seamus and Brandon will take another six after the second. Trust me, boss, we're going to pull this off."

I can't help but feel like everything lately has gone wrong, so trusting this will work out is difficult.

"Okay, so I'll head back to the city." I shake my head. "I ain't being here if this goes wrong." My mind immediately moves to Scarlett and seeing her again. "I want to be kept informed."

Aiden nods. "Of course, sir. I'll provide you updates as and when we have them." He holds out a hand to me, and I take it. "Be careful, all of you," I say, before turning away from my men and leaving them in the abandoned warehouse we rented just outside of Salem.

As I walk out of the warehouse into the parking lot, I know my speedy getaway has nothing to do with being here if things go wrong.

We're finished a day early, and I'm desperate to see my baby girl. I unlock the door to the beaten-up old Mustang that I bought to blend in here. Any of my expensive classic American muscle cars would have been too recognizable here.

Milo Mazzeo hasn't been in Salem, as he's too busy with his political campaign. However, his second-in-command, Piero, has been spotted several times. Important people in his organization are here. It's a bad sign, but I know my men can get the job done.

If they were to kill Milo's capo, then that would be a bonus in my book.

I pull out of the parking lot and drive toward the highway, desperate to get the fuck out of Salem and fast. Ever since we got to the town, I've had a bad feeling I can't seem to shake.

The Italians are smart. All I can do is hope that this time we're one step ahead of them.

Scarlett won't expect me to turn up at her door this afternoon, but I don't care.

It's been a day shy of two weeks since I last saw her —too fucking long. It's clear that I've got it bad for my broken little girl. She's occupied all of my attention when I should have been focusing on the war.

I know that dragging her back to my home is essentially dragging her to the front lines. I'm too selfish not to bring her back home. Milo isn't stupid enough to retaliate at my home. He'd have too many casualties, as the place is like Fort Knox.

It means I will need to keep Scarlett in my home, since Milo has seen her face.

I use my Bluetooth phone system to dial the fanciest restaurant in town, Rare.

"Hello, how can I help you?" a man asks.

"It's Mr. McCarthy, and I need a table tonight."

There are a few moments of silence on the other end as he passes the phone over. "Good afternoon, Mr. McCarthy. Of course, we can accommodate you and your guests. A table for how many?"

I smirk, as there aren't many people in this city that can get a last-minute booking at this place. "A table for two, please, seven o'clock."

"Of course, we look forward to seeing you then."

"Thanks." I cancel the call and focus my attention on the road as I pull onto the highway.

I notice a dark town car following me on the slip road. They've been following me for a few blocks. Once

I'm on the highway, I get suspicious. I monitor the car and drive down the highway until I exit for central Boston.

As I indicate off, the car follows. It can't be a fucking coincidence.

There's a set of lights just off the slip road, and they are red. I slow the car down as if I'm intending to stop. At the last moment, I put my foot down and speed through the lights, dodging a few cars coming the other way.

They honk their horns. When I look in my rearview mirror, the car has followed me.

"Motherfuckers," I growl, slamming my foot on the accelerator and taking the first left down a small side street. If they think that stupid fucking town car can outrun a Mustang, even a shit one, they're wrong.

I take several sharp turns down narrow alleyways. Each time they follow me. My stomach sinks as I hear a bullet ricochet off the car. Thank fuck I wasn't in one of my favorites and was in a banged-up old car I picked up a week ago. Milo has already destroyed my favorite car.

The town car is keeping up better than I expected. I notice a sharp right turn up ahead, knowing it's my only chance to lose them.

I hold off until the very last second before sliding the car sideways. Once the car comes straight again, I slam my foot on the accelerator and head down the alleyway.

The pursuing car doesn't make it and drives straight past the entrance.

I don't lose concentration, knowing if I take one wrong turn, they could catch me.

The next three turns I take are down narrow side streets, keeping off the main roads.

After a few minutes, there's no sign of the black car following me. I take back roads to Scarlett's apartment and park down a side alley. Once parked, I dial Aiden first to warn him about the odd tail I picked up near Salem. I'm sure it had to be the Italians.

"Malachy, is everything okay?" Aiden asks.

"Yeah, just a heads up. Someone tailed me from Salem to Boston. It took me a bit of a chase around to lose them."

"Shit," Aiden says. "Do you think they know about our plans to hit their shipment?"

I shake my head, even though he can't see me. "No, I think they recognized me and tailed me."

Aiden breathes a sigh of relief. "Let's hope so. Thanks for the heads up, though, sir." He clears his throat. "I'll update you as soon as I can."

I cancel the call and then call Mick, my driver.

"Sir, how can I help?" he answers.

"Can you meet me over at Scarlett's house as fast as possible, please?"

I can hear him scrambling around in the background. "Of course, I didn't expect you back until tomorrow."

"As long as you're not drunk, lad, then get the hell over here."

He chuckles. "I'm not drunk, don't worry, boss. I'll be there in fifteen."

"See you then." I cancel the call and get out of the Mustang.

A flower shop opposite Scarlett's building catches my attention. After abandoning her for two weeks, the least I can do is bring her flowers.

I head over to the shop, and the lady behind the counter gives me a strange look as I enter.

The suit and tattoo combination often gets me strange looks. Add in the beard, and people stare all the time.

It angers me, but I let it slide on this occasion. There's a large array of prearranged flower bouquets, and one of them stands out. A mix of white, blue, and red flowers. The blue reminds me of Scarlett's eyes, the red for her fiery hair and the white for her pure innocence.

"I'll take that one, please," I say, pointing at the large bouquet.

The lady's brow furrows, and she picks it up. "It's seventy-five dollars. Is that okay?"

I almost roll my eyes at her. "Yes, thanks." The last thing I want is to cause a scene at a shop opposite Scarlett's home.

This seems like the kind of neighborhood where everyone knows each other. I pay for the bouquet with my bank card before heading over the street to her apartment.

Scarlett has engrained herself so deep under my skin. I know nothing I can do will ever get her out.

The question is, how do I bring up the idea of never letting her go?

I bought her virginity, which I've claimed. There's no reason I should force her to stay, but she hasn't questioned me.

All I can hope is that she allows this to carry on forever. The alternate option is not good.

My dark side won't allow me to let her go. If I break her trust, she'll never look at me the same way again.

19

SCARLETT

I'm sitting on the couch, waiting for mom to return home from her weekend with Frank. They are running late because Frank surprised her with a romantic picnic for lunch.

I'm relieved that she isn't alone, especially since I've got to go back to Malachy for God knows how long.

The doorbell rings, and my brow furrows. I wonder if Mom forgot her keys again. She does that more often than she should.

I get up as the bell rings again. "I'm coming," I say, opening the door.

My heart skips a beat when I see Malachy on the other side, holding a bouquet of red, white, and blue flowers. "Hey, baby girl."

I'm shocked that he'd turn up out of the blue a day early, especially since my mom could have been home. "What are you doing here?"

Malachy looks irritated by my question. "I got back early and wanted to take you to dinner." He's wearing a nice suit, but I'm not sure how I'd explain Malachy to my mom. She could be here any minute.

"My mom is going to be back any minute, and we were going to spend the evening together."

He shakes his head. "It wasn't exactly a question, Scarlett." He nods toward the apartment. "Get dressed for dinner."

I glare into the emerald green eyes of the man whose child is growing inside of me. Every stupid decision I've made since that auction leads to another.

"What if I refuse?" I ask.

Malachy's jaw clenches. "Are you being a naughty girl, Scarlett?" There's a hint of arousal in his eyes, which means my defiance is only fueling his desires.

I shake my head. "Didn't you hear what I said? My mom will be back at any moment. How would I explain you being here?"

He chuckles. "Tell your mom I'm a guy you met who asked you out for dinner. Is it that fucking hard?"

The ding of the elevator stopping at our floor makes my heart skip a beat. Frank and my mom are back.

"Fine, come and wait inside." I grab hold of his arm and drag him inside, knowing he isn't going to leave no matter what I say.

I make sure he sits down as my mom reaches the door. She opens it and stops in her tracks when she sees

Malachy sitting on the sofa. "I'm sorry, Scarlett. I didn't know you had company."

I shake my head. "It's fine. We were going to go for dinner tonight, but then I remembered we're supposed to be spending tonight together. Aren't we?"

My mom waves her hand. "Nonsense. You've spent enough time this week with your boring mom. It's about time you go out and have some fun." She smiles.

Thanks for the save, Mom.

"Who is your friend?" she asks, walking over.

Malachy stands. "My name is Malachy. Nice to meet you." He holds his hand out, and my mom takes it.

"Indeed. Nice to meet you. It's the first time my baby has had a boy around." Her attention moves to the bouquet in his hands. "What lovely flowers. Shall I find a vase?"

Malachy smiles. "Yes, I bought them for Scarlett."

"Right. I'm going to get dressed. I'll be a couple of minutes." I march toward my bedroom and slam the door behind me, leaning against it.

What the hell is Malachy thinking, turning up here?

I was looking forward to a night in with my mom. The last night until Malachy decides to release me from this weird situation that I'm in.

I sigh heavily and throw my sweater and jogging pants on the bed before changing my granny pants for something sexier.

Whether or not I like it, tonight will end in us

having sex. We haven't spent a moment together without it resulting in sex, so I know tonight won't be any different.

I dress in my favorite pair of pants and a gold sequin dress top, wearing a pair of comfortable trainers.

I run my hand through my hair and make sure it's presentable. My makeup is understated, but that's how I like it. Once I'm sure I look okay, but not so good that Malachy won't be able to keep his hands off me, I head back out into the living room.

My heart skips a beat when I see my mom laughing at something Malachy said. They're both sitting on the couch, chatting as if this is natural.

Sure, Mom doesn't know the truth, but Malachy does. He bought my virginity and is now sitting there as though he's a genuine guy coming to take me out for a meal. It's ridiculous.

I clear my throat. "I'm ready, Malachy," I say, my voice stern.

He turns to look at me, and his smile drops. "I don't want to sound like a dick, but we're going to a pretty upmarket restaurant." He runs a hand across the back of his neck as if worried about saying it. "I think you might feel a little more comfortable in a dress, as that's the dress code there."

My mom nods. "Yes, he told me where you are going, and you need a nice dress on." She stands. "How about I help you pick one out, sweetheart?"

I glare at Malachy, wishing he would leave well enough alone. "Fine."

My mom rushes into my room before me, and I follow, shutting the door. "He seems like a lovely man. Where did you find him, Scarlett?"

I shake my head. "I was out, and he asked me on a date." I fold my arms over my chest, wishing that my endless lies would end. It's been lie after lie ever since I met Malachy.

It's ridiculous that my mom thinks he's a nice guy, but she's always been so blinkered about what people are truly like.

I guess that started with my dad, but she's not exactly been the best judge of character after that either. Her best friend of five years stole all of our savings about three years ago and took off. We haven't seen her since.

"How about this dress?" Mom says, holding up one of my sexiest dresses with a low plunging neckline. A dress that Kaia talked me into getting, but I've never worn.

I shake my head. "I think it's too revealing."

My mom sighs. "Sweetheart, I know you're unsure about getting too close to anyone after what happened to you as a little girl." She grabs my hand and pulls me to the edge of the bed. "Believe me, I understand how hard it must be for you, but you have to let someone in." She smiles. "Malachy seems like a nice guy, and you owe it to yourself to give it a serious go."

I nod. "I know, Mom, it's just difficult for me to trust people." If only she knew the truth about the man sitting on our couch.

"Good, now put the dress on."

I sigh heavily and get out of my pants and top, slipping into the dress. "Can you zip me up?"

My mom nods and zips it up, gasping as she looks at me over my shoulder in the mirror. "You look gorgeous, sweetheart." Her smile makes my guilt return with intensity. "I'm so proud."

I want to tell her she shouldn't be proud, not after what I've done. It's stupid to think that I can keep the truth from her forever. Once Malachy finally releases me, I will come clean to her about the entire thing.

How else can I get away with having two million dollars in my bank account?

Despite everything, I wish that I'd met Malachy in different circumstances. My heart almost beat out of my chest when I saw him standing in my doorway with those flowers.

It makes me long for a relationship that could never exist. No serious relationship is born out of the fucked-up way we met, that's for sure.

"What shoes am I going to wear?" I ask, glancing down at my bare feet. I hate heels and don't have any.

"How about these?" My mom holds up an elegant pair of sandals.

I nod. "They'll do." I glance at my mom. "Obviously tomorrow I'm heading back to New York. I might not see you in the morning."

My mom pulls me into a tight hug. "Good luck with the production. I know you'll be amazing." I feel my throat closing up as I realize how bad it's going to be when I come clean about Malachy and the auction.

"Thanks," I murmur before pulling away. "I better get going." I head out of the door and find Malachy leaning against the wall.

He straightens up when he sees me, and his eyes drop down my body in a slow, predatory way that sends shivers down my spine. "You look gorgeous, darlin'."

"She does, doesn't she?" My mom gloats. "Both of you have fun."

I reluctantly take Malachy's outstretched arm, allowing him to lead me out of the apartment.

Malachy turns to me once we're in the elevator. "Your mom seems nice. I don't know what you were so worried about."

I roll my eyes and glance at him. "It wasn't my mom I was worried about. It was you."

He grabs hold of my hips and pushes me against the back wall. "I've missed you, baby girl." I feel the press of his hard cock as he grinds it against me. "Don't act like you didn't miss me too."

I swallow hard, looking into his eyes. "I didn't."

"Bullshit," he says, teasing his hand up my neck and grabbing my throat firmly. "You missed me as much as I missed you." He runs a hand up my exposed thigh and slips a finger into my panties.

I shudder as his finger teases against my sensitive, wet pussy. "No, I didn't—"

Malachy slides a finger inside of me, making me stop halfway through my sentence. "Remember, baby girl. I don't like it when you lie to me," he purrs into my ear, biting my lobe softly. "You're are so fucking wet for daddy."

I feel my body reacting to his heat, his strength. Everything about Malachy McCarthy is intoxicating. His dominance drives me insane.

"Come on, darlin', tell me the truth. Did you miss me?" he asks again, looking me in the eye.

I nod. "Yes, daddy," I reply, feeling myself being pulled back so easily into his dark and dangerous trap. It's the same every time he's near.

He smiles. "That's my girl." He kisses me passionately, making my body melt.

The connection between us is impossible to resist, no matter how much I know I should.

I'm not only lying to my mom, but I'm hiding a secret from the man I've fallen for. A secret I don't know what to do about.

Kaia thinks I should get a termination, but I don't agree with her at all.

The thought of getting rid of a little version of Malachy and me makes me sad, but I can't understand why.

Perhaps it's because I long for something deeper with him. A genuine relationship where he's not holding me captive because he paid me a shitload of money.

I guess a girl can dream, even though that dream will never become a reality.

20

MALACHY

*I*t's tense between us ever since we left her apartment.

I know it's because she's wondering when I'm going to let her go.

Sure, we've only spent just over two weeks together up to now, but that's probably long enough in her eyes.

I forced her to say she missed me, but I'm not sure it's the truth.

When I left her before this war took a turn for the worst, there was an easy air between us. Now, the air is full of tension.

"What are you going to order?" I ask, keeping my eyes on her.

She's barely looked up from the menu since we sat down. "I'm not sure. What do you recommend?"

I smile at her. "Well, since it's a steakhouse. I'd

recommend the steak, medium-rare with the blue cheese sauce."

Her nose wrinkles. "Blue cheese? No, thank you. Who the hell wants to eat moldy cheese?"

I laugh. "I do. It's bloody delicious, and all cheese is mold. Just because you can't see it doesn't mean it's not there."

She shakes her head. "I'm going to get the salmon."

I clench my jaw, feeling irritated that she ignored my suggestion to get a steak. "Are you sure? I think you'll regret not getting a steak here, they're divine."

She narrows her eyes at me. "I'm not into steak much."

I can tell she's being difficult on purpose, trying to wind me up. "Is that right? Well, maybe I'll have to teach you how to like it."

She bites her bottom lip in a way that makes me want to stand up, walk over to her, and take her right here in the middle of the restaurant. My urges are out of control ever since we met.

The waiter approaches. "What can I get for you?"

Scarlett opens her mouth to speak, but I cut in first.

"Two of your best steaks, medium-rare. One with blue cheese sauce, the other with pepper sauce, please."

Her brow furrows, and she opens her mouth to protest.

"We'll also get a salmon en croute."

The waiter looks confused now. "Is that to share?" he asks.

I nod. "Yes."

Scarlett folds her arms over her chest and sits back in her seat, looking flustered. "I'm not sure how you think I'm going to eat a steak and half the salmon."

I shake my head. "I don't expect you to." I sip my glass of scotch, watching her over the rim. "You can eat what you want. We can take home anything we don't finish."

Her eyes widen when I mention home. "Where is that then?" she asks.

"I hadn't mentioned it yet, but I thought it would be obvious that I intend to bring you back to mine tonight."

She nods. "Okay."

I'm surprised she doesn't put up a fight. "What have you been doing since I last saw you?"

Scarlett sighs. "Not a lot. It's been boring, since I don't have a job anymore."

"Did you enjoy spending time with your mom?"

She nods. "Yes, the doctors say she's doing great, and they think she's already entering remission." Scarlett smiles the first genuine smile since I picked her up. "It's the first time in a while I've seen her so positive." Her eyes meet mine, and I feel a spark ignite between us. "It's all thanks to you."

I swallow hard. "You mean because I'm a sick bastard that bids on virgins at auctions?"

Her gaze hardens, and she nods. "Basically."

I know she wants me to accept her thanks, but I

have done nothing. She put herself up for auction. If I hadn't bid, she still would have been able to save her mom. She'd probably be back to her day-to-day life.

Although a few of the guys who bid on virgins often have to bury the girls. I've heard about it more than once.

It's sick to think that some of those men end up killing the girls. I thought I was fucked up, but I've never killed a virgin.

"What have you been doing?" she asks, lifting her glass of water and taking a sip. It's strange that she hasn't even touched the glass of wine I ordered for her.

"Working hard to stop Milo from getting the better of me." I run a hand across the back of my neck, feeling the tension in my shoulders build just thinking about it. "The Italians are proving a tough opponent to strike back at."

Her brow furrows. "Then, why are you here with me tonight?"

I sigh. "Because we've finally found a way to hit them, and my men are doing it tonight." My cell phone rings as if talking about my men summoned a damn call from them.

"We were successful but had a couple of casualties," Aiden says.

I'm thankful to hear of the success. "Any fatalities on our side?"

Aiden is silent. "Not yet, we're hoping the few injuries won't prove to be life-threatening."

"Good. Keep me in the loop. Great work, Aiden." I cancel the call. "Sorry, it was one of my men."

"Sounds like its good news." Scarlett says.

I chuck back the rest of my whiskey and slam the glass down on the table. "Yes, but what isn't good is this sudden distance between us, darlin'." I get up from my side of the booth and sit next to her. "Are you mad at me?"

Scarlett can't look me in the eye as she looks down at her lap. "No, I just…" She trails off and doesn't finish what she was going to say.

I grab her hand. "Look at me, Scarlett. What's wrong?"

She shakes her head. "Nothing, I just don't understand what is happening between us."

"That makes two of us, darlin'." I run my hand down her thigh. "Can't we enjoy getting to know each other and not think about it?"

Scarlett looks a little disappointed about my suggestion to sweep the issue under the carpet. "Sure."

The waiter returns with our food, clearing his throat. "Two steaks and the salmon en croute, sir."

I stand and return to my side of the table. "Yes, thanks." I hold my empty glass up. "Another Irish whiskey, please, lad."

He takes the empty glass from me and goes to get me another. The way Scarlett is acting, I'm going to need half a bottle of whiskey to get me through this night.

"Why aren't you drinking your wine?" I ask, noticing she still hasn't touched it.

Her cheeks redden, and she shakes her head. "I don't feel like drinking tonight."

Suddenly, I wonder if she's been out partying any of the nights she's been back. Why else would she not want to drink?

"You better not have been going out drinking while I was away, Scarlett."

She sits up straighter and searches my eyes. "What if I have been?"

I feel a possessive rage infecting my blood at the mere thought of her being groped and dancing with other men at a club. "I'll be angry."

Scarlett rolls her eyes, making that possession grow inside of me. "Don't be stupid. You didn't give me any rules before dumping me back home."

I growl and slam my fist down on the table, making her jump. "Scarlett, tell me the truth. Have you been out with other men while I've been gone?"

Her eyes widen, and she stares at me like I'm insane —maybe I am. "No, for fuck's sake." She shakes her head in disbelief. "I don't want to drink. Is that a crime?"

I breathe deeply, trying to get a handle on my over-whelming rage. I can sense that something has changed between us since the last time we were together.

If another man has weaseled his way into her heart,

I'll have to kill him. I won't stand by while someone steals my woman from me.

"Did you buy any virgins while I was home?" she asks, a hint of sarcasm in her tone.

I narrow my eyes at her and ignore the question. "Eat your food before it gets cold."

She tucks into her steak and puts a small piece into her mouth, undeterred by my angry outburst. "It is a pretty good steak, even though I'm not that into steak."

I feel some of my rage ease. "I told you it was good, darlin'."

Scarlett's eyes widen as she looks behind me. "Isn't that the guy from the Italian restaurant?" she asks.

I glance behind me and see Milo scanning the restaurant, no doubt searching for me. How he knew I was here, I'll never know.

It suggests that they've got a tracker in Mick's car.

I duck under the table. "Get down now, baby girl."

Scarlett doesn't question me as she joins me under the table, eyes wide. "We're in danger right now, aren't we?" she asks, voice so quiet and small.

"Keep quiet, and we'll be okay." I don't know that for certain. After the shit my men pulled on his shipment, Milo won't be merciful if he finds us.

I think as fast as I can, trying to work out what the best plan is. Milo is a bastard, and he won't be too fussed about making a scene in public.

The man is ruthless, and I won't let him get his hands on Scarlett. There's no way he'd think seeing her with me twice is a coincidence. He'll want to hurt her the way I hurt his wife.

"What are we going to do?" Scarlett asks.

I run a hand over my beard. "Maybe we can dash out of the back of the restaurant?" I suggest.

Scarlett nods. "We're close to the back. Should I check where Milo is?"

I shake my head. "I will." I turn around and pop my head up enough to allow me to scan the restaurant, seeing him over the other side. "This is our best chance." I grab hold of her hand. "Are you ready?"

Scarlett nods, and I get up, pulling her with me.

We make a quick and quiet dash for the back door, pulling it open and almost colliding with a waitress.

She shrieks, and I dodge around her fast, knowing the sound would have drawn Milo's attention.

"Move fast, Scarlett. He'll be after us now."

Scarlett lets go of my hand, and we both sprint toward the fire exit at the back of the kitchen. I lead the way, knocking people out of it as I go. My heart is hammering at a thousand miles an hour.

In hindsight, coming out for dinner on the night my men were stealing a shit load of cocaine was a bad idea. At least now I know there's a security leak linked to Mick's car.

The fire alarm sounds the moment I slam through the door, glancing back to check Scarlett is behind me.

I feel a flood of panic when I see Milo entering the

restaurant kitchen, eyes frantic. "McCarthy, stop," he growls.

I'm not sure why the idiot is chasing me, as last time we faced each other, he ended up beaten and shot. The only reason I'm running is because I'm with Scarlett. I won't risk her in such a dangerous situation.

As soon as Scarlett makes it through, I slam the fire door shut and grab her hand. "Quick, we need to find a cab fast."

We run down the street, heading toward a cab with its light on. I open the door and force Scarlett inside before getting in. "We need to get to Beacon Hills."

The cab driver nods. "No problem. What's the address?"

I tell him the address and instantly relax when I feel the cab pull away from the curb, thankful that we managed to getaway.

When I glance back out of the window, I can see Milo looking in every direction. He chucks something on the floor in anger, knowing that he lost us.

I pull my cell phone out of my jacket and type a text to Mick.

Your car is compromised. Ditch it and get back to base.

That was too close for my liking. I won't risk Scarlett like that again, not while this war is raging.

21

SCARLETT

I feel sick when we finally get to Malachy's home—so sick that I'm sure I'm going to throw up.

Sure enough, the moment I get out of the cab, I throw up on the sidewalk. Malachy pays the cab driver, who comments that I'm a good sport for waiting until I got out of the cab.

Malachy grabs hold of me and supports me toward the gates. "Are you okay?"

I shrug. "Yeah, I think it's the adrenaline that got to me," I lie, knowing that it may well have something to do with the baby I'm carrying.

The thought of telling him about it makes me sick to the stomach. I feel my stomach churn, and I wonder if I'm going to throw up again.

"You look pale, Scarlett. Maybe you need something to eat?" Malachy suggests.

"Unfortunately, our expensive dinner is on the table back at the restaurant."

Malachy chuckles. "Don't worry. I'll get takeout delivered. What do you want?"

I think about what I could stomach right now, which is not a lot. "Pizza?" I ask.

Malachy nods. "Whatever you want, baby girl." He helps me through the front door and leads me down a corridor I've never been down before.

A door on the right opens to a cozy little room with a large television at one end and a big plush sofa at the other. "Milo might have ruined our date, but I'll make sure you still have a good time tonight, darlin'."

I hate the way my stomach flips every time he calls me that.

"Sit down and rest. I'll order the food and get us some drinks."

I grab hold of his hand. "No alcohol for me, please." I shake my head. "I can't stomach it, and I need to brush my teeth."

He smiles. "I'm not stupid. You just puked. I'll get you a fruit smoothie, and there's a new toothbrush in the adjoining bathroom." He nods toward a door in the corner of the room. "Knock yourself out."

I bite my lip, wondering if this could ever be our lives. Malachy and I living together in his mansion with a child or two. It's a stupid notion. One that makes little sense considering the way we met.

His sister's remark by that lake that day has stuck with me.

I wish Malachy would settle down with a nice girl like you.

I wish he would too. Although not with a girl like me, but with me. I want him to be mine the way he claims I belong to him. I stand up and head into the bathroom, finding the new toothbrush in the cabinet under the sink. There's a tube of unopened toothpaste in there too. I'm thankful to freshen up and head back out to find Malachy sitting on the sofa.

I sit down next to him.

"Here we go, one fruit smoothie." He passes me the drink. "And pizza will be here within half an hour."

"Thank you." I try to take the drink, but he doesn't let go.

"Thank you, what?" he asks.

My stomach flips, and my thighs shake as I know what he's expecting from me. "Thank you, daddy."

He smiles and lets go of the drink. "Good girl." He wraps an arm around me, pulling me toward him.

The heat of his body and the masculine scent of whiskey and pine make me feel safe. I nestle into him, enjoying being back in his arms. "I missed this," I murmur.

Malachy tightens his grip. "So did I, baby girl." He presses a kiss to my forehead. "I don't think I'm ever going to be ready to let you go."

My chest aches and I feel happy hearing him say

that. "I don't think I want you to," I whisper, so quietly I'm not sure he'll even hear me.

He pulls away from me and looks at me, searching my eyes. "Do you mean that?"

I nod in response, forgetting for a moment about the secret I'm keeping from him. "I think so." I search his emerald green eyes. "Is that crazy?"

Instead of answering me, Malachy kisses me passionately. The kiss steals the breath from my lungs as his tongue forcefully searches every inch of my mouth.

There's a change in the way he touches me. It's possessive and rougher, even though he's always been tough. His fingers dig hard into my hips as he forces me to straddle his lap. I feel the hard press of his cock beneath me.

Malachy is forceful as he holds me down, restraining me with my hands behind my back. "It's been too long since I was inside of you," he murmurs, pressing his lips to my neck.

"What about the food?" I ask.

"Fuck the food. I'm hungry for you, baby girl."

I can't deny that I feel the same. The past two weeks have been torture not seeing Malachy. It feels different now that I'm keeping a secret from him. I can't bring myself to terminate the baby, even if Kaia thinks it's the best option.

"What are you thinking?" He asks.

I shake my head. "Nothing."

He smirks against the column of my throat. "Liar."

I swallow hard, as there's no way I'm telling him what I'm thinking.

I feel his teeth graze against my skin. "Maybe you are looking for a punishment, darlin'."

I feel my body react to the suggestion of him punishing me. My panties dampen at the thought of him taking me in hand. "What kind of punishment, daddy?"

He bites my collarbone. "I'm going to introduce you to a darker side to BDSM." He kisses my jaw before pressing his lips to mine again. "I hope you're ready."

I swallow hard, wondering what he might be talking about. "I do too."

He lifts me and sets me down on the large couch before walking away. "Wait here while I fetch a few things."

My brow furrows as I watch him walk out of the room, leaving me to overthink what he means by a darker side of BDSM.

He returns after a few minutes with a hell of a lot of rope, some strange-looking implements, and a vibrator. My thighs quiver at the thought of him using any of it on me.

"Strip for me," he orders.

I stand from the sofa and undress, feeling as nervous as I did the first night we spent together. It doesn't help that the pregnancy is always on my mind.

"Shut your eyes, darlin'," Malachy drawls.

I clench my jaw as the difficulty to trust rules me,

but I shut my eyes, anyway. I feel a piece of fabric over my eyes and open them to find he's blindfolded me.

"I'm going to tie you up next," he says, making my stomach churn.

The thought of him taking away both my sight and freedom to move makes me even more anxious.

"Malachy, I'm not—"

He wraps his fingers around my throat, stopping me. "You know the rules, baby girl. You do as I say, and if anything gets too much, you have the safe word."

I let out a shaky breath, trying to calm myself. The man I'm with hasn't given me a reason not to trust him up to now, but my past makes trusting difficult.

Malachy ties me up, wrapping the rope around me so many times. It's a strange sensation as the ropes offer pressure over my entire body, making me feel vulnerable.

"I'm going to lower you to the sofa," Malachy says before using the ropes to gently lower me.

I swallow hard, wondering what to expect next. Although I can't see, I can sense Malachy close to me. There's some rustling as I keep my thighs clamped together.

"Legs open," Malachy orders, his voice harsh.

I swallow hard and open my thighs to him. My heart skips a beat when I feel him clamping metal chains around my ankles. "This bar will ensure you can't close them at all."

I think he forgets that I'm blindfolded and can't see

what bar he's talking about. When he claps the other ankle in the strap, I feel what he means. A pressure keeps my legs spread, making it impossible to close them.

Losing control makes me panic for a moment, but I breathe deeply, remembering that I'm with a man I trust. It may sound crazy that I trust a criminal, but I do.

Malachy's fingers clamp around my throat suddenly, lightly blocking my airways. "Do you remember the word?"

I nod in response, feeling a tightening in my chest at the darkness in his voice.

"Good." Suddenly, I hear the buzz of the vibrator. It sends my pulse racing. Malachy says nothing as he gently places the rubber against my inner thigh, teasing me with it.

I shiver as he moves it slowly closer to my pussy. The anticipation is overwhelming as he gets close, only to move it to my other thigh. I'm practically gushing everywhere by the time he finally places it against my aching clit.

The vibration feels like fire, setting me alight inside and out. "Fuck," I moan.

Malachy growls a low, throaty noise and slaps my inner thigh with something firm. "No dirty words, baby girl."

I swallow hard, feeling my nipples tighten at the sound of his rough voice. "Sorry, daddy."

He returns the vibrator to my skin, teasing me again. I'm so desperate to feel the sensation between my thighs, but he's making me wait as punishment.

When I auctioned my virginity off to this man, I did not know what to expect. I assumed I would spend one night with the bidder before going home in the morning.

The last thing I ever expected was to feel myself falling prey to my buyer's charms. The sheer amount of trust I'm giving him now to have free rein over my body proves that this has become so much more than a business transaction.

He gently brushes the vibrator through my soaking wet folds, making me moan. When it hits my clit, my entire body shudders. Malachy backs off instantly, making me unbelievably frustrated.

I bite my lip when I realize I'm on the edge of begging Malachy.

"I want you to beg me for it, darlin'," he says, making the hair on the back of my neck stand on end. It's as if he read my mind.

My stomach churns as he continues to tease me, placing the vibrator on my thighs. Slowly, he moves it toward my pussy.

"Beg me, Scarlett."

I bite my lip, feeling embarrassed that he's made me so needy I am about to beg. "Please, daddy."

The cane comes down hard on my right thigh,

making me yelp. "What the——" Another strike on my left thigh silences me.

"Please what, darlin'?" There are a few moments of silence between us as I try to work out what he means and get over the pain he inflicted without warning. "I want you to be specific when you beg me."

"Please make me come," I say. My voice sounds raw.

He groans above me before returning the vibrator to my thighs, where he'd hit me. The mix of pain and pleasure is intoxicating. It astounds me I enjoy what he's doing. "If you're a good girl, then I'll let you come. Do you understand?"

I swallow hard. "Yes, daddy."

He moves the vibrator closer to where I so desperately need it. I grunt in frustration when he pulls it away a little, continuing to tease me.

"Please let me feel it on my clit, daddy," I beg, shocked by the needy sound of my voice. It doesn't sound like me anymore.

Without a word, he does as I ask. My entire body jerks at the intense vibrations pulsing through me as he moves it in circles around my aching clit. "Yes, daddy, yes," I cry, feeling the muscles spasm as he sends me over the edge so fast. It feels like I'm free falling without a parachute. The intensity of the orgasm is so raw it floods my vision with sparkling white light. For a moment, I wonder if I died.

Malachy's strong, rough hand gently teases around

my throat. "You're such a dirty little girl, Scarlett," he says, his voice more detached. "And dirty little girls need to be punished."

My entire body quivers at the word. "What kind of punishment, daddy?"

He tightens his grip around my throat. "I'm going to put you over my knee and cane that perfect, round ass of yours until you're red and raw."

My stomach churns. It almost sounds violent. I can't work out whether I'm excited about being punished or scared. Malachy grabs hold of the bar between my legs, slipping an arm around my back, flipping me over.

I feel him maneuver himself so he's beneath me. His hand cups my soaking wet pussy hard, making me groan. "So wet for me, baby girl," he purrs.

I cry out as the cane connects with my right ass cheek first, sending a terrible pain stinging through my flesh. "That hurts," I cry out, toying with saying the safe word. He struck me harder than he did on my thighs, so hard I'm sure it will leave bruises.

"You know the rules, darlin'. If you want me to stop, you know the word." His reminder soothes my fears a little, proving I have an out. The word will get me out of this if it gets too much for me to handle.

I stay quiet, waiting for more punishment.

He brings the cane down on my left ass cheek harder. I swallow the cry of pain, feeling tears prickling at my eyes. A dark part of me feels like this is what I need. A strong, dominant hand to guide me. All my life

I've felt like I've been floating along with no purpose or sense of direction.

Malachy knows how to give me direction, discipline, and above all, care.

The next few strikes are harder again, making me writhe over his lap in pain. My thighs still spread wide apart, but I can feel the heavy press of his cock against my stomach.

He plunges two fingers deep inside of me in between strikes of the cane. "Naughty girl," he says, plunging his fingers hard inside of me. "You are so wet. I think you're enjoying this punishment a little too much."

I can feel the pressure inside of me building as he thrusts in and out, curling his fingers in a way that hits the right spot every time.

He pulls his fingers out of me, and then the cane replaces them, coming down softly on my pussy. The sensation is painful and pleasurable at the same time. Each one heightens the other in ways I never could have imagined in my wildest dreams. "I think I'm going to come," I cry, feeling confused by my receptiveness to pain.

Malachy growls. "I didn't tell you to come yet." He canes my ass harder than ever, but all it does is push me over the edge.

My entire body shakes with intensity, and I feel the wet liquid gushing from my pussy and down my thighs. "I'm sorry, daddy. I couldn't hold it."

He growls like a savage beast and lifts me off his lap, dropping me on the sofa on my back. "It's because you're my dirty little whore, and I'm going to fuck you so hard the household will hear you screaming."

There's a manic sound to his voice, making me wish I could see his face. The blindfold makes me feel so unaware of his emotions. "Are you going to take the blindfold off?"

Malachy grunts before yanking it away from me. "Only because I want to look into your eyes while I fuck you harder than ever before."

There's an equally manic look in his eyes when I meet his gaze. He already has his shirt off, revealing his lean muscles covered in dark, scrolling ink. A sight that makes the desire heighten and my nipples so hard they hurt.

He pulls the belt from his pants, dropping them to the floor. All he's wearing now are his tight boxer briefs wet with cum, framing his huge, hard cock perfectly.

He watches me like a hawk as he drags his boxer briefs down, revealing his big dick. He's dripping with cum and ready to take me. A deep ache unlike anything I've ever felt ignites inside of me—an ache to be filled with him.

Malachy strokes his cock and sets a hand on the bar between my legs. He bends his knees, so his cock is in line with my dripping pussy, and pushes forward, filling me to the hilt.

I moan so loud I think he's right. The entire house-hold will hear us tonight. I've craved this moment since he left me outside my apartment almost two weeks ago. When we were separated, it felt like I was no longer whole.

He watches me like a hawk as he moves in and out, hard but slow at first. The sound of our skin clashing together fills the room. I stare into his eyes, almost mesmerized by the beautiful emerald hue of his pupils. "I own you, Scarlett," he murmurs, staring right back. "You belong to me in every sense of the word." There's possessiveness in his declaration—a possessiveness that makes me feel special.

"Yes, daddy," I say.

We're both lost to each other. Our bodies become one as we give in to our tortured needs for one another. I know as he fucks me roughly that this man is the only man for me. He may be a criminal, he may be a savage, but he's my savage.

"Harder, please, daddy," I beg, allowing my walls to melt away.

Malachy growls. "I never knew you liked it so rough, darlin'." He starts to fuck me harder, pounding me into the sofa so hard I think I might break. My ankles are up high, and the spreader bar keeps me wide open for him.

My pleasure is building as I watch him move above me. His emerald green eyes hold mine with an intensity that only deepens my connection with him. It doesn't matter how hard I try to resist it. Malachy is made for me.

When you know it's right, you know.

Malachy and I are right in every sense of the word, no matter how screwed up the circumstances are.

Malachy pushes me higher and higher, his cock pounding into me so hard I think he's going to break me in two. I writhe against the restraints around my wrists, wishing I could grab hold of something.

"I want you to come for me, darlin'," he drawls.

His scent, his voice, his cock, everything about him drives me insane. I feel myself on the edge, ready to explode. My vision blurs, and I know I'm about to come. "Yes, daddy, I'm coming," I cry.

For the third time tonight, Malachy tips me over the edge. I scream so loud I think the household will have heard me, even in this huge, cavernous place. My body spasms, revolting against the bindings and the spreader bar, keeping me firmly in place.

"Fuck, baby girl. I love feeling you come on my cock," Malachy roars, tipping over the edge with me.

We remain still and panting as we both come down from our mutual pleasure. Malachy finally moves out of me after what feels like forever. He unclips my ankles from the spreader bar, puts my panties back on, and then unties my wrists.

I watch as he walks toward the door, making my stomach sink.

Is he seriously about to abandon me after that?

He returns within a few seconds, holding two pizza boxes. "I think we need to refuel for round two." He shrugs. "Unfortunately, they're cold."

I smile at the man I've fallen for. "I don't mind cold pizza."

He sits by my side, still entirely naked. We sit on the sofa in comfortable silence, eating the cold pizza. I can't find it in myself to care that it's cold, as this is the happiest that I've felt before.

22

MALACHY

M'y eyes open and I notice it's still dark outside. The clock on the nightstand signals its five-thirty in the morning.

I glance down at Scarlett, who is nestled against my side, her delicate hand on my chest.

She shouldn't be cuddling up to me after the way I treated her last night. A perfect, gentle creature like her shouldn't be anywhere near a man like me—ruled by darkness.

I told her I never want to let her go last night, and it's the truth. Scarlett's reaction wasn't exactly what I'd expected. She was open to the idea.

My cell phone buzzes on the nightstand, and I ease her hand off me and roll away to grab it. Seamus's name is on the screen, and I swipe to answer. "Give me one second," I say quietly, holding my hand to the receiver and gently getting out of bed to ensure I don't wake Scarlett.

I walk into the bathroom and shut the door behind me. "What's up?" I ask.

Seamus is silent for a few moments. "It's bad news, boss. Milo has come down hard. He blew up the warehouse at the docks."

"Bastard," I growl, punching the wall so hard that my knuckles will bruise, but the pain is welcome.

My stomach sinks when I see Scarlett standing in the doorway, eyes wide. Her attention is fixed on my knuckles, which are bleeding badly.

"I'll meet you there in thirty minutes." I cancel the call and walk toward her.

Her eyes are still fixed on my bloody knuckles. "You're bleeding." She takes a few steps back before I can reach her.

Her reluctance to be close to me hurts and only serves to fuel the rage building inside of me. "It's nothing." I clench my jaw and take another step forward.

Scarlett takes a step back, keeping the distance between us. "Why did you punch the wall like that?"

It's dangerous for her to be questioning me when I'm in this state. "Don't question me or back away, Scarlett. The worst time to push me is when I'm angry."

There's a flash of defiance in her stunning blue eyes. "Or what? You'll punch me like you did that wall?" She asks, holding my gaze.

I rush toward her and grab her throat, pushing her against the bathroom wall. "I'd never hit you, Scarlett." My rage is taking over at the mere suggestion that I'd ever hurt her, but my actions are only fueling her fear. "Do you think I'd ever hurt you?"

Her eyes narrow. "You already did last night."

I let go of her throat and pace away from her, knowing how dangerous this conversation is. I never intended to scare her off last night, but she hasn't received my rough handling of her well. "You didn't say the safe word, not once." I look at her. "If you didn't enjoy it, why didn't you make me stop?"

Scarlett follows me into the bedroom, crossing her arms over her chest. "I didn't say I didn't enjoy it. You said you'd never hurt me, but that's not exactly true."

I growl. "It's different when it's consensual play." I clench my fists, ignoring the pain tearing through the fist I smashed against the wall. "I'll clarify. I'll never hurt you unless you want me to." I shake my head, scrubbing a hand across the back of my neck. "I've got to get going."

Scarlett looks disappointed by the blunt end to our conversation, but she shouldn't be. It's safer for both of us if we don't continue. I can't trust myself when I'm angry. "Where are you going?"

"Trouble at the docks with Milo." I walk past her, back into the bathroom, shutting the door behind me. There's nothing more to say.

For the first time in my life, I want something real. A

relationship. The hair on the back of my neck stands on end at merely think the word.

It won't end well. The darkness of my past haunts me, and I can't bring that into a partnership with Scarlett.

She needs a man that knows how to be gentle. After last night, I think she learned how savage I could be.

Until last night, our interactions have been pretty vanilla for me. It was stupid for me to think I'd be able to leave behind my rough, dark side. It's ingrained in me, and last night I lost control.

Maybe I've ruined any chance I had with her, anyway. My inner need to inflict pain and dominate took over, and nothing was stopping me.

Scarlett can't have wanted me to stop, though, as she didn't use the agreed safe word. Normally, I don't offer the girls I buy safe words.

It's against the rules of BDSM, but I don't play by rules.

I wash and freshen up, then walk into the closet and change into a loose shirt and pants.

There's no way I'm wearing a suit today. I find it too stifling.

Once dressed, I come out and hear the shower running. Scarlett is in the shower with her back to the door.

My stomach churns as I take in the sight of her bruises on her ass and thighs. I took it too far too fast last night.

It's a surprise she hasn't run out of here as fast as possible. Last night I revealed the monster I truly am. The question is, can Scarlett love a monster like me?

———

It's carnage down at the docks—debris scattered everywhere.

We haven't been stupid enough to use our main warehouse to store our cocaine or guns since the war started.

Instead, I've kept it somewhere no one would ever think to look.

The police are here, and they cordoned the warehouse off with police tape. I walk up to the officer standing guard. "This is my warehouse, lad. I need to go inside."

He looks up at me, rolls his eyes, and returns his attention to a clipboard in his hands. "This is a crime scene. No one is allowed inside."

I grunt in frustration. "I've got important fucking documents in there. I need to check if they survived the blast."

The officer laughs. "Nothing did. Whoever did this has blown the place to pieces and everything inside." He looks up at me again. "Luckily, no one was inside."

I pace away from him, knowing that if I continue to talk to the cop, I'll end up knocking the guy out. A terrible idea when he's a cop. If it were anyone else, they'd be flat out on the floor.

"Boss," Seamus calls to me from one of our nearby warehouses.

I walk to join him and find Aiden, Cormac, and Brandon in there. "Fucking police won't let me inside."

Aiden nods. "It's unfortunate that the blast was so obvious. There was no way the police weren't getting called." He paces toward me. "Luckily, all our cocaine, including the two shipments we stole from Milo, are safe."

They've dealt a public blow to warn us how angry they are. The Italians didn't intend to hurt us financially, as the insurance will payout for damages. Milo intended it as a warning to back off, but there's no chance of that happening. This war is only starting, so it was a desperate move on Milo's side.

It tells me he's not sure how to hurt me yet. My biggest weakness is my sister, but no one outside my inner circle knows it. Scarlett may have quickly become my second weakness. Unfortunately, he knows about her.

It's only a matter of time until he turns his attention to her, especially since he's seen us together more than once.

"What are we going to do about this bastard?" I ask, looking at my men's blank faces.

This is the moment I wish Niall were back to full

health. He's got at least a week until he'll be back to coming to strategic meetings.

He's still living in my basement while he recovers.

"Can't we fight fire with fire?" Cormac suggests.

It's a stupid suggestion. Milo has police connections that would land us in serious trouble if we committed such a public crime. "We don't have the sway with the cops like the Italians do."

I walk into the warehouse and run my hand over one of the old steel industrial benches. "Why don't we try to take Milo's wife again?" I suggest.

Seamus shakes his head. "The guy has her under lock and key. She's harder to get to than his fucking cocaine, and that's saying something."

I run a hand across my beard. "She must leave the house?"

Cormac nods. "Yes, with three bodyguards every single bloody time since this war started." He narrows his eyes. "The guy must care for her or just doesn't want to be made to look weak again."

There's no doubt in my mind that Milo cares for the woman he married, even if it was by an arrangement. The anger I saw in his eyes when I threatened her was enough of a giveaway.

"I have a better idea," Brandon says, surprising us all, as he's normally the one to keep quiet.

"What is it then, lad?"

I can tell from the look in his eyes that his idea is

going to hit the Italians hard. "I've heard a rumor that Milo is bringing a lot of cargo from Sicily."

I almost roll my eyes. After his deal with his wife's father, Fabio Alteri, that's common knowledge. "Yes, everyone knows that."

Brandon nods. "But do they know that the ships he sends are too large to dock in Salem? He's struck a deal with Enzo D'Angelo to bring all shipments directly into the New York docks."

I narrow my eyes at Brandon, wondering where he's going with this. "I didn't know that, but what is your point?"

"If we can intercept his next drop from Sicily in the ocean, we will land much more than we did the other day, chasing his containers."

It's a fucking insane idea. An idea that would mean taking the war to the sea.

Seamus clears his throat. "That could work, other than it's crazy."

Aiden laughs. "It's insane, but we could pull it off, but the fallout will be huge." He runs a hand through his hair. "Fabio Alteri won't be too impressed either, so we might end up fighting a war on both sides of the Atlantic."

I nod. "Yeah, pissing off the Sicilians is a bad idea." I run a hand through my beard. "It's a risk we'll have to take if we want to hit them hard. Get it set up."

Brandon looks surprised I took his suggestion seriously, but he's a clever kid. The youngest in my trusted circle of men, but still a good kid.

"I heard about the explosion. The doctor has signed me off to come back."

I smile at the sound of Niall's voice. "Welcome back, lad." I turn around and walk up to him, pulling him into a hug. "I'm glad you're back in time for the most epic plan ever."

He raises a brow. "What kind of plan?"

"We're going to take out Fabio's shipment before it even lands on American soil."

Niall's brow furrows, and he shakes his head. "That's a bad fucking idea, Mal."

I grit my teeth, hearing him call me Mal. "For fuck's sake, you're back one minute and immediately blow the wind from my sails."

He laughs. "You would start a war with Enzo D'Angelo and Fabio Alteri." His brow furrows. "Do you think we can fight a war against three Italian crime organizations?"

As always, my much-needed voice of wisdom returns. I tend to be hot-headed and take unnecessary risks when he's not around. "Not really, but how else can we strike back for this stupid fucking move?"

Niall smiles. "It looks like I came back at the right time." He sighs. "There's a high-stakes casino night at Milo's casino in the center of the city tonight. All of his top men will be in attendance." There's an evil glint in his eyes. "I say let's blow it up and end this shit once and for all."

A sense of pride swells in my chest as I stare at my second-in-command. My best friend. "What the hell would we do without you, Niall?"

He shrugs. "End up in a war you can't win, it would seem."

"Okay, we run with Niall's plan as it's perfect." I stop for a moment and glance at him. "How did you find out about the casino night?"

He shrugs. "I heard about the high-stakes casino night from an informant on the inside."

"Good work." I clap him on the shoulder. "You best get in touch with Patrick and get the explosives we need fast, planting them there before tonight."

Niall nods. "On it, sir." He turns away and heads out of the warehouse.

"The rest of you, wait for instructions."

"Aye, sir," they say in chorus before dispersing.

I notice Aiden lingering behind. "Boss, can I have a word?"

I nod and walk toward him. "What is it, lad?"

He pulls out a piece of paper. "Regarding the man you wanted me to find. The father of Scarlett Carmichael."

I clench my jaw. "Yeah, did you find him?"

He nods. "He's serving ten years at a state penitentiary in Massachusetts."

My brow furrows. "Are you sure? The guy was from

Texas." I hate to think that bastard that exploited my girl is breathing in the same state as her.

"Positive." He rubs a hand across the back of his neck. "They sent him down for sexually abusing his daughter with a woman he married here only five years ago."

I nod. "Thanks for looking into it." I take the paper from him. "Leave this with me."

There's a questioning look in Aiden's eyes, but he doesn't ask why I'm looking into this guy. It frustrates me I can't be the man to slit his throat. The risk is too great. Going into a state prison in Massachusetts and hoping to get away with it would be a certain prison sentence. However, I know a guy inside who will do it for me willingly.

They call him *The Slasher*. I know him as Darragh as he's my only living cousin now that Milo killed his two brothers. The guy is crazier than me, and that's saying something. It's time to visit my cousin.

23

SCARLETT

I stare at myself in the mirror, wondering if I know who I am at all anymore. Last night I allowed Malachy to treat me like a slave, and I liked it. A sick part of me wants this to continue, even though I know how broken he is.

The bruises on my body are superficial, but they're proof of how savage the man I've sold myself to can be. I enjoyed the way pain and pleasure blended. Now, as I stare at the dark marks on my skin, I'm wondering if I'm truly broken.

This morning I should escape this house and never looking back, but my heart is vested in whatever this is between us. I towel dry my hair before getting dressed into some loose clothes that hide the bruises.

I glance at the invite the housekeeper dropped in after Malachy left. Alicia has invited me to have breakfast with her this morning. It'll be the second time I've seen her since Malachy ambushed us in the woods.

I feel nervous, and I think it's because of the bruises. Alicia mentioned I was less beaten up than the rest of them. Will she know the truth now? Malachy bruised and marked me too.

I shake my head and finish towel drying my hair. Once satisfied with my appearance, I walk toward the door. When I open it, my heart skips a beat. Alicia is standing in the hallway wrapped in the arms of a large, tattooed man whom she is kissing passionately.

"Morning," I say as they are blocking my way down the corridor.

They both jump apart as if I've burned them. "Morning, Scarlett," Alicia says, eyes wide. "Are you ready for breakfast?"

I nod in response. "Sure, is your friend joining us?"

The guy shakes his head. "No, I was just leaving." He turns and walks down the hall stiffly, without another word to either of us.

"Who is that?" I ask, looking at the concerned look on Alicia's face.

She shakes her head. "No one. Come on, let's get something to eat. I'm starving." She hooks our arms together, and we walk in a tense silence down the hall.

I can tell she's lying about that guy. They both didn't want to get caught together. Instead of pushing it, I let it slide, as it's not my business what Malachy's sister is up to.

The kitchen table is already laid out with lots of pastry, bread, and jams. "This looks delicious," I say, breaking the ice.

Alicia smiles. "Yeah, Lianne is an amazing cook. She makes these pastries from scratch." She picks up a croissant and breaks some off, popping it in her mouth, then sits down at the table.

I sit opposite her, trying not to wince as the hard chair connects with my thoroughly bruised ass.

Alicia doesn't notice my discomfort, or at least she says nothing. "How have you been?"

I shrug. "As well as can be expected."

Alicia nods. "Yeah, my brother is a barbarian." She narrows her eyes at me. "Yet, you still are faring a lot better than any of the others." She breaks off more of the croissant and eats it. "Maybe he intends to keep you around."

My stomach flutters at the suggestion. The words Malachy said to me before our evening took a rather dark turn have been playing like a broken record in my head.

I don't think I'm ever going to be ready to let you go.

My heart had almost exploded when I heard him say that. I even told him I didn't want him to, but the discussion didn't get any further. Something tells me that Malachy isn't the kind of man who ever considered settling down or having children.

"Are you okay?" Alicia asks, looking at me with concern. "You seem a little spaced out."

I nod. "Yes, I'm fine." I shrug. "It's been a little crazy ever since the auction. I didn't know what I was signing myself up for."

Alicia laughs. "None of the virgins my brother buys ever do, but then you haven't had the treatment a lot of them have had."

I feel my stomach twist. I'm curious to know what exactly he did to the other girls. "What do you mean? What exactly did he do to them?"

Alicia looks a little reluctant but speaks. "He tortured them both mentally and sexually. It's pretty fucking disgusting since he's my brother, and by the time he's through with them, they probably need serious therapy."

There's a tense silence that falls between us.

"Although, I know it's because of the shit he went through as a kid." She looks a little torn, staring at her half-eaten croissant. "I love my brother as he's protected me since we were children, making sure I was safe even when we lived on the streets." She sighs. "Unfortunately, the sacrifices he made as a child have darkened him in ways I can never understand. He shielded me from the darkness, and for that, I'll be eternally grateful."

I nod in response. "It sounds like you both had it rough growing up." It makes my story with my father seem tame.

"Yes, the worst of it was in the foster care system. The system landed us with the worst couple ever, who sexually abused Malachy the entire time we were there." She draws in a long shaky breath. "He always protected me from any abuse from them. On the night we escaped, he had to knock the guy out to stop him from raping me." She shakes her head. "The system is fucked up. We were safer out on the streets than with the psychos who were supposed to provide us a safe home." Alicia breaks out of her daze and meets my gaze. "Whatever you do, don't tell him I told you all this." She runs a hand through her pretty dark hair. "He wouldn't be happy with me."

I smile. "Don't worry. I won't tell." I'm curious about how he ended up going from the streets to running an illegal organized crime group and living in a multi-million-dollar mansion. "How did you get from the streets to here?"

"Malachy is one tough bastard," she says, shaking her head. "He started bare-knuckle fighting on the streets against people twice his age, winning fight after fight. In the end, he became the champion, and this gave him enough money to get us off the streets."

I remember the way he beat that man who almost raped me while I walked home. He was savage. I can believe that he is a champion fighter after witnessing that.

She shrugs. "From there, my brother built a group of men around him. Niall was his best friend on the streets, and he became his second-in-command. Malachy built the clan and started taking control of territory off of the Italians and Russians. It wasn't easy going, but he built it with his bare hands, and although it's not legal, I couldn't be prouder of what he has achieved."

I nod, as it's quite a feat to overcome such hardship and end up on top the way he is. "How old is Malachy?"

Alicia shakes her head. "You've been sleeping with him for over a month now, and you don't know his age?"

I shrug in response.

"He's forty-two years old."

My stomach flips as he's older than I thought—eighteen years older than me. He looks younger, in his early thirties perhaps. I grab a chocolate croissant from the platter on the table and eat some of it. "I thought he was in his thirties."

Alicia shakes her head. "No, it's a McCarthy family trait: looking younger than we are." She tilts her head to the side slightly. "How old do you think I look?"

I had always thought she was in her late twenties. "I hope this is right. I thought you were about twenty-nine years old."

She puts a hand to her chest. "I'll take it. I'm Thirty-Six going on Thirty-Seven in a month."

My eyes widen. "Wow, yeah, it runs in the family." She no way looks like she's in her late thirties.

A comfortable silence falls between us as we both eat. I'm glad for the company this morning as often my days are so boring being forced to stay in Malachy's house, but they were boring while I was at home too.

"What was your job before you auctioned your virginity?" Alicia asks.

I feel ashamed that it was so pitiful. Despite all the help that my mom gave me to get the best start in life and follow my dream, I've failed miserably. Malachy started with nothing and pulled himself up to the top. "I was a waitress, but I've always wanted to dance professionally."

Alicia claps her hands. "I love dancing. Maybe we can go dancing together sometime?"

I smile at her enthusiasm. "Yeah, maybe once I'm released from Malachy's prison."

"It isn't too bad of a prison." She grabs the pot of coffee and pours herself some. "How much did he pay for your virginity, anyway? I've always been curious as to the price he pays but never asked him."

I feel my face heat, and guilt twists my stomach. "Malachy bid two and a half million dollars."

Alicia's eyes widen. "Fuck. I didn't know he paid that much." She shrugs. "But that's a good thing. It means you can get your mom the best medical care possible."

I nod. "Yeah, but I feel dirty about how I got it."

She holds the coffee pot up. "Coffee?"

I pick up my cup and move it toward her. "Yes, thanks."

"You shouldn't feel guilty for doing whatever it takes

to get your mom the medical care she needs." Alicia shrugs. "I'd do it for my family." She laughs. "If I were still a virgin, which I'm definitely not."

We both laugh at the irony since I caught a man sneaking out of her room this morning. The easy conversation flows as we spend the morning talking about our lives and interests.

There's no doubt that I get along with Alicia. I wonder what it would be like if Malachy did settle down with our baby and me. Alicia would be an aunt and a great one at that, I'd bet.

It's a silly fantasy. Malachy may have said he never wants to let me go last night, but it was in the heat of the moment. Our pent-up frustrations after not seeing each other for two weeks all collided. I know he can't feel that way.

A happy ending with Malachy and me having a family is not in the cards. No matter how badly I wish it could be.

24

MALACHY

*M*y cousin is in the same jail as Scarlett's dad. I hate visiting the prison, as it's a reminder of where I could end up if things ever went south with the clan.

Darragh ended up in prison because he's a psychopath. He murdered seven women during sex before being sentenced to life. There's no way he'll ever see the outside of the prison so long as he's alive, but he thrives in an environment full of chaos.

I sit, waiting for him to enter on the other side of the glass. The entrance into the holding area opens, and he strolls in. His dark eyes are almost onyx black. Even I fear my cousin, and I don't fear many people. He's not right in the head and never has been.

When he was eight years old, he stabbed a girl in his class with a pencil right through her hand. His violent tendencies only spiraled out of control from there.

Darragh smiles at me and picks up the phone. "Little cousin. It's good to see ya."

"Good to see you too, Darragh." I run a hand across the back of my neck. "Look, I need a favor."

His eyes narrow. "What kind of favor."

I hold up the picture of Scarlett's dad and the small write-up about him to the glass.

Darragh skims it. "Consider it fucking done. I hate people that mess with kids," he growls.

I fold up the paper and place it back into my pocket, thankful the guards didn't notice. "Thank you. How is everything?"

He shrugs. "As good as it can be when you're locked up for fucking life," he says.

I nod. "You still running this place?"

He smiles. "Always." Darragh has taken over the supply of drugs entirely inside the prison. I guess it runs in the family.

My father's brother was always a worthless drug dealer. However, I've elevated his position ever since the McCarthy clan took control of the Irish quarter of the city. My father was different. He and my mother both ran their legitimate businesses. If my mom hadn't died in childbirth, things would have turned out differently.

Not that I'd have it any other way. If things hadn't happened the way they did, then Alicia wouldn't be here. She's the world to me, and I'd never change that.

"You'll call me when it's done?" I ask.

Darragh nods. "I'm itching for a kill, Cousin. I will do it before you get home."

I smile uneasily, but inside I can't help but wonder what goes through his head. Despite having to kill in my life many times, I'd never say I'm itching to murder. I do what is necessary to keep my legacy alive.

"I'll expect a call from you soon then."

Darragh stands. "It was good to see you, Cousin." He winks. "Tell my father and brothers that they are pieces of shit for never coming to visit."

I swallow hard. "Ah, that's something I need to tell you."

Darragh stops walking and returns to the booth we're in. "What is it?"

I know how insane Darragh can be when he's angry, but it should only help him carry out the murder on Scarlett's father. "Oisin and Sean were both killed by the Italian bastard, Milo Mazzeo."

Darragh punches the glass between us, but it's toughened. He can't break it. "Motherfuckers." I can tell from the look on his face he's about to lose his shit.

The guard comes toward him. I watch as he tackles one guard to the ground. In the end, four guards have to hold him down and restrain him.

I don't wait any longer, knowing there's no use hanging around. It's about time I get back to the city and get ready for tonight's takedown.

SCARLETT'S LAUGH hits my ears the moment I step into my home. It carries down a corridor, and I instantly wonder what bastard is making her laugh. A fit of hot, possessive jealousy sweeps through me.

I march toward the sitting room. The same room we fucked in last night. When I round the corner, the possessiveness instantly dies down. Alicia and Scarlett are sitting together watching a comedy film. A strange pang in my chest ignites, seeing the two most important women in my life getting along.

I lean against the doorframe and watch them for a short while before clearing my throat to get their attention. "What is going on in here?"

Scarlett jumps at the sound of my voice, but Alicia rolls her eyes. "We're watching a movie. What does it look like?"

Scarlett's attention is no longer on the movie, but entirely on me.

"Is that right?" I glance at my watch. "Well, unfortunately, Scarlett is going to have to miss the end of the movie."

Alicia shakes her head. "Can't you jerk off or something?"

I narrow my eyes and feel a pulse of rage at the suggestion that all I want Scarlett for is sex. "We have a function to attend tonight."

Scarlett sits up straighter. "What kind of function?"

I run a hand through my hair, hesitating. The debate over whether or not to bring Scarlett tonight has been warring in my head ever since I left the docks. "A high-stakes casino night."

Her brow furrows. "I guess I'll need to find something fancy to wear then?"

"Yes, come with me. I've already arranged something."

She glances at Alicia, who waves her hand as if to say it's fine. "I'll catch up with you later," my sister says.

I can't deny that Scarlett hanging out with my sister makes me nervous. Alicia has a big mouth, and after what she told her about my past last time, it wouldn't surprise me if she's given her more detail now.

I don't want Scarlett to know about the abuse I received in foster care. It's a wound that won't heal and festers beneath the surface, feeding the darkness within.

"What have you two been talking about?" I ask once we're out of earshot of Alicia.

Scarlett looks up at me and shakes her head. "Too many things to list. We spent the day together."

I grit my teeth. "Did I give you permission, baby girl?"

She shakes her head. "No, but the invite came after you left. I couldn't contact you to ask."

I stop walking. "Give me your cell phone."

She gives me a questioning look but obeys. I open the contacts and add my number to her phone. "You've got my number now, so that's no excuse in the future."

Scarlett nods in response. "Okay, daddy," she says obediently, placing my phone back in her pants pocket. Hearing her call me daddy makes my cock hard, but I know we have no time to indulge my desires.

I lace my fingers with hers and lead her toward my bedroom. "I've got something special for you to wear tonight." My cock throbs at the thought of her in the exquisite blue evening gown I chose.

I open the door to the bedroom and lead her inside, shutting the door. The garment bag has been left on the back of the bathroom door by my housekeeper, as instructed.

"Why don't you look?" I ask, nodding at it.

Scarlett walks slowly toward the bag. Her hesitation is endearing. She unzips the bag to reveal the royal blue evening gown adorned with silver sequins. "It's beautiful," she says, her voice full of awe.

I walk up behind her and wrap my arms around her waist. "It's not as beautiful as you." I press my lips to the back of her neck, feeling her shiver against me. "There's this to go with it too." I hold out the box in front of her, keeping her back against my chest.

She tries to glance over her shoulder at me, but I hold her in place. "What is it?" she asks.

"Open it and find out."

For a moment, she does nothing. After a few seconds, she flips open the lid of the box to reveal a pair of diamond drop earrings and a matching pendant.

Scarlett gasps. "They're stunning."

I smile against her neck. "They're yours, darlin'."

She shakes her head. "You mean to wear tonight, right?"

I spin her around to face me. "No, they're a gift for you to keep."

"They're too much." Her eyes fill with what I can only describe as guilt.

Her refusal of my gift angers me. "Bullshit. If I want to give you a gift, then I'll damn well give you a gift." I grab hold of her hips possessively, pulling her toward the long mirror on the wall. "I want you to strip for me so that I can dress you."

Scarlett pulls off her sweater and pants obediently. She stops there, forcing me to give more instructions.

"Lingerie off too."

Scarlett unhooks her bra and drops it to the floor before stepping out of the skimpy black thong she was wearing.

I let my eyes move down her body slowly, halting the moment I see the bruises on her thighs. I clench my jaw as a flood of guilt washes through me. The sight is a reminder of how rough I was with her last night and our argument this morning.

I set the jewelry box down on a chair and walk back for the garment bag, pulling the dress out of it. All the while, Scarlett watches me carefully.

"What about underwear?" she asks, eyeing the dress as I return to stand behind her.

I shake my head. "No underwear tonight." I unzip the dress and hold it in front of her.

Scarlett steps into the dress, and slowly I pull it up her perfect body. The bruises are worse on her ass, and it makes the guilt increase. I cover them with the royal blue fabric, finding the dress fits her like a glove. I zip her in before turning my attention to the box I set down on the chair nearby.

I fetch it and return to stand behind Scarlett. "Tonight is going to be dangerous." I slide the necklace around her neck and do up the clasp.

Scarlett watches me the entire time in the mirror before gently touching the necklace and staring at herself in awe. "Dangerous?" she asks.

I can't believe how stunning she looks. It's clear she doesn't realize how beautiful she is. I nod and pass her one earring to put in. "Yes, we're going to Milo Mazzeo's casino."

The change in her countenance is obvious. I notice the worry etched into her features. "Why?" she asks, meeting my gaze in the mirror.

The plan is insane, but it's the best option we've got. "Tonight, we are going to end this once and for all. My men have rigged the place with enough explosives to level it." I pass the other earring into her hand.

Her brow furrows. "So why the fuck are we going in there, then?"

I can't help but laugh. "If we make an appearance, then it rules my men and me out of the investigation."

"Surely, it'll be more likely that they'll see you as guilty if you leave before the blast?" She questions.

"We won't be leaving before the blast. I know what part of the building is safe from destruction." I run a hand over my beard. "We will be there when the explosion goes off and lucky to survive."

I notice Scarlett pale and place a hand on her stomach. "Are you sure that's a good idea?"

It's the best idea we've got to work with. "Believe me. We will live. I guarantee it, darlin'." I pull her around to face me. "You've got nothing to fear." My desire rules over me as I press my lips to hers, kissing her passionately.

I try to ignore the niggling doubt at the back of my mind. The plan is insane, but I know it's the best way to limit casualties and end this war once and for all. Milo thinks I'm too weak to take him out, but that's not true.

Assassinating him in cold blood would cause tensions to heighten, but an explosion which can't be linked to the McCarthy clan that wipes out most of his men will strengthen our position.

Knowing that I'm taking my most precious possession into a very dangerous situation, I break the kiss. "We better get going, or we will be late," I murmur against Scarlett's lips.

It's impossible not to notice the tension in her shoulders. I entwine my fingers with hers, pulling her toward the door. Adrenaline is pulsing through my veins as I walk us right into a dangerous situation.

I will protect Scarlett, no matter the cost. The question is, am I taking too many risks to win this war?

25

SCARLETT

*M*alachy gets out of the Impala first and walks around to my side, opening the door.

He looks unbelievably handsome in a tuxedo. "Are you ready?"

I can't believe that we're about to walk into the lion's den, which is rigged with explosives. Malachy insists it's necessary and that Milo wouldn't expect such a public attack. Malachy reckons that once all his enemies are dead, there won't be anyone to come after him. The cops are shady and take bribes from the Italians mostly, but Malachy intends to swoop in and take their place once they're gone.

"I'm not sure," I say quietly, knowing my biggest reservation is that I'm pregnant. It's not only my life on the line.

He smiles at me and shakes his head. "Don't worry,

darlin'. I'll protect you." His lips tease against my shoulder. "Always," he murmurs.

I hate the way my heart rate speeds up at that word. This man knows how much I've fallen for him. It's cruel to toy with someone's emotions the way he constantly toys with mine. The sensible part of my brain tells me to cut my losses and get away from Malachy fast. However, my heart doesn't agree.

I smile and shake my head. "I'm not worried."

He sets his hand lower on my back and guides me toward the entrance. "Milo will approach us, so just act natural when he does."

"Okay, I still don't understand why we're making an appearance." It seems insane that we're walking into a casino rigged with explosives.

"I told you, it's the only way to ensure the attack isn't pinned on me." Malachy leans towards me. "After tonight, Milo won't be breathing any longer, and I don't want to get the blame."

The guard at the entrance steps into Malachy's way. "This event is invite only. Do you have an invitation?"

He stands taller, removing his hand from my back. "Do you not know who I am, lad?"

The guy stares at him blankly. "It doesn't matter who you are if you don't have an invitation."

I can sense Malachy's irritation. "Get Milo out here now."

The bouncer's brow furrows. "You know Mr. Mazzeo personally?"

"Yes, I don't think he'll be impressed that you kept out his acquaintance, do you?"

The guy looks around nervously before stepping aside and nodding. "Go on in then."

Malachy guides me around him, and I'm surprised how easy it was to get in without an invitation. "I wasn't sure he was going to let us in," I whisper.

"He would have let me in. The men who work here don't know the truth about their boss and his underground organization as far as I'm aware." We walk up to the cashier's desk. Malachy buys chips to the value of five hundred thousand dollars.

"Are you intending to bet that much money?" I ask once we leave the cashier.

"Yes, it's a drop in the ocean." Malachy smiles but doesn't look at me as he speaks. He is searching the casino.

I follow his gaze and notice the Italian don standing with his back to us at the roulette table. A stunning, elegant woman stands by his side with dark curling hair running down her back. The same woman who was with him at his restaurant.

"Who is the woman he's with?" I ask.

Malachy meets my gaze. "His wife."

I'm surprised to hear he's married. "What is the plan, then?"

Malachy smiles at me and leans toward my ear. "Time to gamble, baby girl."

I swallow hard, knowing he doesn't just mean with

money. Out of instinct, I place my hand on my stomach, remembering that it's not only my life on the line here. Malachy might not have dragged me along to this if he knew.

We walk straight over to the table Milo is at. "Is there room for another player?" Malachy asks.

I notice the way Milo and his wife both tense at the sound of his voice. "Who let you in here?" he asks, his ice-blue eyes narrowing in on Malachy.

Malachy shrugs. "The guy on the door." He runs a hand through his short hair. "I'm surprised you didn't invite me, to be honest."

Milo's eyes narrow. "You have some balls coming in here, McCarthy." Milo's arm possessively wraps around his wife, who is staring at Malachy with such fear. It makes me wonder what on earth he did to her the last time they met. "Unless you came to agree on a truce."

"I came to gamble." He nods at the croupier. "Deal me in." He sets his chips down on the table.

The croupier glances at his boss, Milo, for permission to allow him to play. Milo nods reluctantly, and the tension in the air is so thick that it is stifling. The dealer spins the wheel. "Place your bets," he announces.

Malachy takes twenty thousand dollars' worth of chips and places it on red.

Milo takes two times as many chips and puts it on black. It makes sense that he'd bid on the opposite. They are enemies.

We are all silent as we watch the wheel spin. "No

more bets," the dealer announces as the ball and wheel slow down. I can feel all of us holding our breath, waiting for the ball to stop. It feels like a lifetime until the ball lands on red eighteen.

Malachy smirks as the dealer calls it and pays him out twenty-thousand dollars in winnings. He glances at me. "Your turn now, darlin'."

Milo is watching him like a hawk. "Aida, why don't you have a go," he says, not even glancing at his wife.

I stare up at Malachy, wondering how he expects me to play. Tonight is the first time I've stepped inside a casino, let alone seen anyone play Roulette. "I don't know the rules."

"It's easy. Place a bet on something on the board, like red or black, or odd or even." He pauses a moment. "If you feel lucky, you can bet on a specific number and color."

The thought of losing Malachy's money makes me nervous as he passes twenty-thousand dollars' worth of chips into my hand. The dealer spins the wheel again. "Place your bets," he calls.

I stare at the board, overthinking what I'm doing. I don't want to lose Malachy's money. I place it on evens, and Aida makes her move after me, placing it on red. Thankfully, we're not going head-to-head, and I notice her offer me a small smile. I feel she's not as much of a dick as her husband.

The tension increases as the wheel slows. I hold my breath, waiting to see if I've lost twenty thousand dollars. An insane amount of money. The ball stops on red thirty-four.

"Well, look at that. We both win," Aida says, smiling.

The dealer pays out the chips to both of us.

Milo claps his hand, making me jump. "Let's stop with the child's play and up the stakes, McCarthy."

Malachy straightens up. "What do you propose?"

He grabs a stack of four larger chips. "Two hundred thousand dollars on the next bid each."

I watch as Malachy smirks at the suggestion. "No problem." He picks up the same amount of chips and places them on the board but not in position. "Bring it on."

Milo's eyes narrow, and he nods at the dealer, who spins the wheel. "Place your bets," he calls.

Malachy is the first to move, putting all of his money on black.

The next move Milo makes is predictable as he puts his two hundred thousand dollars on red. I can't believe that these two men barely bat an eyelid when gambling with such sizeable sums of money. Malachy is rich, and so is Milo, but I can't comprehend the level of disposable income they have.

The wheel takes longer this time to slow, but it's probably my imagination. When it finally stops, my stomach sinks. Red number three is what the ball lands on, meaning Malachy lost.

A muscle in his jaw ticks, but it is the only sign that

he's irritated by losing. I feel it's not because of the amount of money he lost, but who he's playing against.

Milo is smirking, and his wife looks as concerned as I feel about this entire situation. "Too rich for your blood, Malachy?" he asks.

Malachy shakes his head. "Not at all. I'm ready to go again." He nods at the dealer who is about to spin the roulette wheel.

"Well, what do we have here?" A man with an eastern European accent asks. "I think I need to get in on this action."

"Who the fuck is in charge of my security tonight?" Milo asks, eyes wild with rage. "Whoever he is, I'll kill him with my bare hands."

"Mikhail, what an unpleasant surprise," Malachy says.

He merely glares at Malachy before taking a position at the table. "I could say the same, McCarthy."

I give Malachy a questioning look, but he shakes his head.

"Carry on, dealer," Mikhail says, waving his hands at him.

The dealer looks a little flustered at the tension in the air, clearly unaware of the insane criminal underworld that exists. I feel that Mikhail is an enemy of both Malachy and Milo.

He spins the wheel and announces they can place their bids. Mikhail places his bet first, putting an insane amount of chips down on black. Malachy bids on even numbers, and Milo bids on red, going head-to-head with Mikhail this time.

The three men stare at the wheel, willing it to land in their favor. It's clear that the competition has nothing to do with gambling and everything to do with the dynamic of their relationships.

The dealer swallows hard as the ball lands on twenty-two black, meaning Milo lost this time. Milo clenches his fist as Mikhail doesn't even smile as he collects his winnings. Malachy looks pleased.

I can't wait for this to be over. The tension among these three men is too much to handle.

All I want is to get our baby and me far away from danger before we're blown to dust and ash.

26

MALACHY

I check my watch, noticing the time. "It was great playing with you two, but I'm going to try my hand at another table," I say, tapping the table for the dealer to deal me out. Mikhail's surprise appearance has thrown the entire plan down the drain, and I need to inform my men it's off.

The dealer nods, and I collect my chips. As I move to leave, Milo dares to grab hold of my forearm. "I have instructed my men to keep close tabs on you. If you try anything, they won't hesitate to kill you."

I meet the Italian's glare. "I'd like to see them try." I tear my arm from his grasp and slide my hand onto Scarlett's back. "Come on, darlin', let's get something to drink."

Scarlett clings to my arm as we walk toward the bar. "That was intense."

I laugh. "Believe me. I've been in tenser situations with Milo. That was tame if you ask me."

Scarlett looks irritated. "Do you mean the last time you two met that you won't tell me about?"

I clench my jaw, feeling angry that she is bringing that up again here. "I won't tell you about it because I was a fucking savage that day." I meet her questioning gaze. "You wouldn't look at me the same way if you knew."

Her brow furrows. "How would you know?"

I shake my head. "This isn't the time or place to have this conversation." I slip my hand from her back to her hip and squeeze. "I need a drink, and we're running out of time to stop the plan, darlin'. The fact that Mikhail Gurin is here means we have one big fucking problem."

It seems my reminder of the coming explosion snaps her back to the matter at hand. "Who is he?"

I run a hand across the back of my neck. "Russian mafia and not the kind of guy I wanted to kill in this blast. I need to stop it before it's too late, or the Russians will annihilate us."

I set my attention on the mayor who is here tonight, no doubt because Milo is to become the next city council member. The entire city council will be done away with tonight if all goes well. He's standing at the bar with his wife, talking to Jameson, of all people.

When Jameson notices me approaching, his eyes

widen. "Malachy, I didn't expect to see you here tonight."

The mayor turns to face me. "I'm sorry, I don't think we've met." His eyes narrow as he notices the tattoo visible over the collar of my shirt.

I shake my head. "No, I don't think we have." I hold my hand out to him. "Malachy McCarthy, successful entrepreneur in this city."

The mayor smiles and takes my hand. "I see, like Milo then?"

I nod in response. "You could say that."

Jameson gives me a warning glare. "Can I get you something to drink, Malachy?"

"Irish whiskey, and…" I glance at Scarlett, realizing I don't know what her favorite drink is yet. "What would you like, darlin'?"

"I'll have a water, please."

My brow furrows that at such a high-pressured moment, she chooses water. "Don't be silly, Scarlett. You can have a proper drink."

Scarlett's cheeks flush. "I'm thirsty and just want water, please."

Jameson nods and turns to the bartender. "One water and one Irish whiskey, please."

This isn't the first time she's turned down alcohol lately, and that's when something hits me.

Could she be pregnant?

We've been messing about for over a month, but we

weren't together for two weeks. The girl wound me up so much that I didn't make sure she was on the pill when I fucked her. I got the pill for all the virgins before her to ensure there would be no unwanted shocks.

Jameson passes us our drinks. "Thanks, if you would excuse us for just a moment." I steer Scarlett away from the crowd and down a quiet corridor.

"What's going on? Is this where we need to be?" Scarlett looks at me, and her face pales when she notices the rage on my face.

"Don't tell me you're pregnant, and you kept it from me."

Her face pales, and she takes a step back. "What?"

I shake my head, hating the way she tries to play dumb with me. "Tell me why you're not drinking alcohol."

She searches my eyes for a few long moments before letting out a shaky breath. "Yes, I am pregnant." She takes a step away from me, putting some distance between us. "While we were apart, I took a test."

It feels like the news knocks the breath from my lungs. *Pregnant.* There's no way I'm cut out to be a father. "Why didn't you tell me when I picked you up that night?"

She keeps her eyes down. "I didn't know how to tell you or how you would react."

I lift her chin and force her to meet my gaze. "You should have told me before we came in here." I shake my head. "You're pregnant with my baby, darlin'. Didn't you think I had the right to know?"

She nods. "Yes, I was scared that—"

"Scared I'd force you to get rid of it?" I ask.

Scarlett doesn't understand the depth of my feelings for her, thinking I'd ever make her terminate our child.

She shrugs. "Maybe."

The anger I feel that she would think I'd ever ask her to get rid of our child is uncontrollable. I punch the wall, busting open my knuckles. "You are fucking insane, Scarlett. Why the hell would I ever ask you to do that?"

She searches my eyes as if looking for the answer to an unspoken question.

"Don't you know how much I care about you?" I ask, searching her eyes right back.

It's as if we're both scared to take that last leap and tell each other the truth. The truth I've known for a long time. Scarlett is the one for me. The love of my life and soul mate, even if I believed I didn't deserve to find either. She can heal the wounds I thought would never heal deep inside of me—hell, she's already started to heal them.

"I hoped, but I never…" she trails off, unsure how to express herself.

A man walks down the corridor, breaking the tension between us. I realize that this is not the time or place to be having such an intimate and important conversation.

"Boss, we got your text. What is going on?" Niall speaks through the earpiece.

I hold a finger to my ear and hold up my receiver. "Mikhail Gurin is in the building. It's as simple as that."

"Fuck," Niall says in response. "Fair enough, we will abort for now." There's a few moments of silence. "What about the explosives?"

I realize how dangerous it is to leave them to be discovered at a later date by Milo's men. "Leave it to me."

"Sir, be careful and get out of there as soon as you can."

I say nothing more. "What's going on?" Scarlett asks.

"Since Mikhail is here, we've had to abort the plan."

Her brow furrows. "He is one of your enemies too. Why don't you let him go up in smoke?"

I sigh heavily. "I wish I could, darlin'. Mikhail Gurin is a powerful man with unbelievably powerful friends up and down the country." I run a hand across the back of my neck. "Including Andrei Petrov, the pakhan of New York City Bratva." I shake my head. "The Russians are smart and form inter-city alliances. If Gurin dies, then Petrov would be here in a heartbeat. We can't risk the heat."

Scarlett looks a little confused as I grab her hand and lead her to a table in the bar. "I don't have time right now to teach you the politics of this world. All I want is for you to stay here while I do some damage control. Can you do that for me?"

"Yes, daddy," she says quietly, making me aroused at the most inconvenient time. It's crazy the power this woman has over me.

I press my lips to hers in a soft, quick kiss. "Good girl. I'll be back as quick as I can. Don't move from this spot."

I turn away from her and head down the corridor, further into the building. We rigged the explosives below us to the left-hand side, right under the main gambling area. Scarlett is in the bar, which is the safest part of the building if they were to explode.

The corridor is deserted, which is a good sign. It's going to be a tougher feat trying to get into the basement without being seen. My heart kicks up speed as I hear footsteps coming from the other way toward me.

Fuck.

If I have to knock some Italian bastard out, then so be it. Three men round the corner and fix their attention on me as if they expected to see me here. "McCarthy, isn't it?" One of them asks.

My brow furrows. "What is it to you, lad?"

He shakes his head. "If you wanted to get your explosives. They are long gone."

My stomach sinks. "I don't know what you're talking about."

One man smirks. "You know what we're talking about. We found them before the night even started."

My mind returns to Scarlett. They have me here, and they won't hesitate to snatch her or hurt her while I'm incapacitated. "I don't know what you guys are talking about, but I'm out of here." I run for it back toward the way I came, only to collide with a wall of solid muscle.

"Not so fast, pretty boy." It's the bouncer who allowed me in at the entrance. The entire time this has all been a setup. They knew what I intended to do from the start.

I punch the guy hard in the face, breaking his nose. If they think they'll take me down without a serious fight, they're wrong.

The guy grunts as I push away, dodging around him and rushing back toward the main casino. All the while, the only thing I can think about is Scarlett and the danger she's in.

I slam the door into the main casino shut. A broom left nearby is perfect for sliding through the handles of the door to hold it shut long enough for me to lose them. I take a calming breath and walk casually across the casino floor toward the bar, despite the panic I'm in to run to Scarlett.

When I get to her table, there is no sign of her. At that moment, crippling panic hits.

Milo has his hand on the love of my life. I know that the only hope now is to find her and save her before it's too late. After the way I treated his wife, Milo won't hesitate to harm Scarlett as badly. He'll kill her if he gets the chance.

I scan the casino floor, searching for any sign of my red-haired beauty. I've not been this scared since I was a kid in that foster home. Scarlett means everything to me, and I can't lose her.

27

SCARLETT

*T*he bathroom is vacant. Although Malachy told me to stay in the bar, I needed to get out of the casino.

He was angry when I told him I thought he might have forced me to have an abortion. I didn't know how to tell him I was pregnant. The door to the bathroom opens, and my stomach dips when I see Milo and two other men standing behind me.

I turn around, trying to remain calm. "This is the ladies' bathroom."

Milo laughs an evil, cruel laugh that sends shivers down my spine. "Is that right, bella?"

I dash for the nearest cubicle, but Milo is too fast. He grabs me by my waist and hoists me away from it. "Let go of me," I cry, trying to kick myself free.

One of his men assists and holds my legs still. They

set me down on my feet so that they can cage me against a wall.

I swallow hard, wondering where Malachy is.

"Did you and your boyfriend think you could come in here and blow the place up and get away with it?"

My heart stops beating for a moment. Milo found out Malachy's plan. "I-I don't know what you're talking about."

Milo smirks, and it's one of the cruelest smiles I've ever seen. Malachy is dark, but this man is pitch black. I can tell he delights in my fear. "Cut the crap with me, bella." He moves forward, closing the gap between us. "We found the explosives before the night began and disarmed them."

I feel my back knock into the wall and realize at that moment that I'm trapped. "What do you want?"

Milo stops advancing and tilts his head to the side. "Revenge on that sick and twisted son of a bitch that seems to have you on a leash." He narrows his eyes at me. "I bet he hasn't told you what he did to my wife when he kidnapped her less than two months ago."

My stomach twists as I realize I'm about to find out from this man what Malachy wouldn't tell me. "What did he do?"

I can tell by the evil glint in Milo's eyes that he's enjoying this. "He had his men kidnap her from Boston Logan International Airport and then tortured her at a warehouse of his." Milo steps closer to me, making me increasingly aware of how cornered he has me. "He cut her with a knife, making her bleed." Milo shakes his head. "Luckily, I found her quickly. Otherwise, he told me what he would have done. He told me he would have raped her before killing her."

My stomach twists at the thought. Malachy can't be capable of such darkness, can he? I know that darkness drives him in ways that I can't fully understand. Malachy had no one to look out for him, the way my mom looked out for me. If it weren't for her, maybe I'd be as fucked up as he is.

"That can't be true," I murmur.

Milo laughs. "Believe me, it's true." He glances over at one of his men. "Since I'm a happily married man, rape is off the cards for me. Piero will happily do the honors, won't you?"

The man he addressed, Piero, looks reluctant. "If it's an order, boss."

Milo looks disappointed. "Are you telling me you don't want to fuck this pretty little redhead?" His attention moves to the other man. "How about you, Angelo?"

The other man smirks and moves forward. "I'm definitely up for it." He runs a hand across the front of his pants, making me sick to the stomach.

Malachy told me not to leave the bar. He'll be searching for me but won't find me until it's too late.

The door of the bathroom swings open. Piero is pulled back and smashed into a wall, hard. Malachy stands over him with frantic, wild eyes. "Get the fuck away from my girl, Milo."

He slams the other guy, Angelo, into the wall too, knocking him out cold.

Milo laughs and grabs hold of me, pushing me in front of him. "Or what? The tables have turned since last time, haven't they?" He runs a hand across my chest, making my stomach churn. "Pretty girl you've landed here. Shame I have to defile her the way you defiled my wife."

Malachy growls like a beast. "You fucking dare, and I'll kill you with my bare hands."

He laughs. "Not before I snap your woman's neck."

Cold dread slices through me as I realize how dangerous the man holding me is. I don't doubt that he would kill me without hesitation to hurt Malachy. They're enemies, and Malachy hurt his wife. I feel an eye for an eye is the general rule these men play by.

"What do you want, Milo?" Malachy asks, admitting defeat.

"Do you think you have anything to offer me, Malachy?"

Malachy steps closer, making Milo pull his knife. Milo places the knife hard against my throat. This seems like an impossible situation with no escape. "An end to the war and your coke returned by midnight?"

The pressure of Milo's knife eases. "There's no way you'd call a truce this easily. What's the catch?"

Malachy glances at me for a prolonged moment, as

if trying to communicate something. When his gaze dips lower, I get the drift. He wants me to fight.

Milo's attention is no longer fixed on me as he watches his enemy. "Well, spit it out. What's the fucking catch, McCarthy?"

I free my arm and bring my elbow into his crotch, hard. "Cazzo," Milo cries as he lets go of me long enough so that I can run over to Malachy.

"The catch is it's a bullshit offer, Milo." I grab hold of Scarlett and push her behind me. "Why does this feel a lot like déjà vu?" Malachy asks.

Milo chuckles. "I've been brushing up on my fist-fighting skills since last time."

Malachy moves toward him, making me nervous. "That's good for you, but it won't help." I watch as he lifts his hands in front of him. "Are you ready to lose again, Mazzeo?"

Milo's nostrils flare as he brings his fists in front of his face. "I'm ready to beat you this time, McCarthy." The testosterone in this room is too much. It's ridiculous how self-assured these two men are. I guess that's how they have to be to run mafia organizations as they do.

Alicia mentioned Malachy has been bare-knuckle fighting from a young age. I'm confident that he can defeat Milo.

My heart skips a beat as Milo strikes first, punching for his left side.

Malachy dodges the swing easily and brings his fist up in an uppercut, catching Milo's chin.

It's a blow that hurts Milo as he retreats backward, grabbing his jaw. "That's a mean fucking upper-cut you have on you."

"You don't become an undefeated champion without one," Malachy says, now on the offense as he steps toward Milo, punching him in the gut.

Milo grunts and lashes out in anger. "Fucking Irish bastard," he growls, punching Malachy in the stomach.

I wince, wondering if it hurt him. Malachy appears to be entirely unfazed by the blow and moves toward Milo without hesitation. "Is that all you've got?" He shakes his head. "I'm not sure you've been brushing up on fist fighting enough." He punches him three times, catching him in the stomach, then jaw, before returning to his stomach again.

Milo retreats for the second time, seemingly unable to get away in such a confined space.

"This fight is only going to end one way," Malachy continues to taunt him, making him angrier. The angrier Milo gets, the more mistakes he makes.

Milo growls and rushes toward Malachy. He lands a couple of hard punches, but Malachy shakes them off.

I hate watching him get hurt. My mind returns to our conversation before he went to sort out the explosives.

Don't you know how much I care about you?

I never allowed myself to believe that Malachy could feel anything for me. The way we met was anything but traditional. Surely, a love story can't blossom out of such an unusual situation.

As I watch him fight to save me, I know deep down that we both love each other. We may be emotionally detached and broken, but we care for each other. I can't imagine my life without Malachy in it, no matter the danger that follows him.

I gasp as Milo lands a nasty punch on Malachy's face, but he hardly notices it. Malachy is so tough. It's hard to believe how someone can be like that.

I'm in awe of him, and although I'd never tell him what Alicia told me, I can't believe he found so much strength after what he's been through. Some people break from hardship, and others rise out of it stronger and brighter than ever.

Malachy's past may have damaged him, but he owns it in a way I never could. He never had the chance I had to heal the trauma he experienced, and from the sound of it, he experienced a lot more than me.

"Is that the best you've got?" Milo taunts as Malachy lands a punch to his ribs.

Malachy doesn't react. He merely continues to move around his opponent. It's elegant the way he moves, a bit like a dancer.

He waits for the opportune moment before striking Milo so hard he cuts open his eye. Blood drips down Milo's face as he tries to stay focused on Malachy.

Something tells me that this fight is going to get

bloody before it ends. I'm not worried whether Malachy will win, I'm worried that he might murder Milo.

He certainly can kill with his fist, as I've seen it first-hand before. If Malachy kills him in cold blood, there's only one place his going and that is jail.

MALACHY

I punch Milo out cold with the winning hit. As I stare at his limp body on the floor of the ladies' bathroom, the temptation to end him here and now is immense.

The manhunt that would ensue wouldn't be worth it. It had to be impossible to link Milo's death to me and killing him with my bare hands is the opposite.

I reach for Scarlett's hand. "Come on, darlin'. Let's get the fuck out of here."

Scarlett glares down at the unconscious man on the floor. "Aren't you going to kill him?" she asks, shocking me with the bluntness of her question.

I smile at her and shake my head. "No. If I were to kill him in cold blood, you could bet all the money in the world that I'd end up in prison."

"That's true." Her gaze softens as she meets mine. "We best get out of here, fast."

It's only at that moment I realize one of Milo's men has entered the bathroom.

"Not so fast." He holds his fists out in front of him.

I force Scarlett behind me and beckon for him to come closer with my hand.

He hesitates, proving that he has no idea what he's doing when it comes to fist fighting.

I step forward and punch him square in the jaw. He groans in pain, trying to bring a hand to where I hit him. Before he can, I punch him in the stomach. The force knocks the wind out of him, and he collapses to his knees, gasping for air.

I reach for Scarlett's hand and finally drag her out of the bathroom, but that's only the first step. This place is crawling with Milo's guys, and we need to get out.

"How are we going to escape?" Scarlett whispers.

I shake my head. "I'm trying to work out a plan, darlin'."

Scanning the room, I notice an emergency exit on the far side. "The emergency exit is our best bet, but we'll have to remain undetected on our way over to that side of the room." I nod over to it.

Scarlett looks pensive as she scans the room. "We're going to have to chance it."

"I agree." There's no other choice but to get to the exit without being seen by Milo's men. I may have knocked Milo out, but he won't be out for long. "Let's go." I lace my fingers with Scarlett's and lead her across the casino floor.

We make it halfway across with no problem until Mikhail Gurin steps into our path. "Malachy, where is Milo?"

I shrug in response. "How the fuck would I know? I'm not exactly on good terms with the guy."

His eyes narrow in on my bloodied fists. "You fought him and won?" he asks.

"Yes, what is it to you?"

Mikhail runs a hand across the back of his neck. "Trying to work out which man to back in this war. At the moment, you're proving the most resilient." He holds out a hand to me, and I eye it warily. The Russians are sneaky bastards, and with their inter-city alliances, their power isn't something to laugh at.

I take his hand and shake it, knowing that pissing off another of the Boston criminal elite would be a bad idea. "I intend to keep it that way."

Mikhail nods and steps out of my way. "You better get going, as I can see Milo."

My stomach churns, and I resist the urge to gaze over my shoulder. "Has the bastard spotted me?"

He shakes his head. "Not yet. Go."

Scarlett tightens her grip on my hand, reminding me it's not only me I need to save. Her life and our baby's life are at risk if I can't get her to safety.

We continue our way toward the escape route slowly. If we were to run, they'd notice us easily.

Thankfully, the casino is full of so many people, it's easy to blend in.

We make it a few feet from the fire exit when Milo's wife steps in front of us. "Where do you think you are going, Malachy?"

I stare straight into her eyes threateningly, knowing that no matter how brave she tries to act, I scare her. "I'm leaving, Aida." I narrow my eyes at her. "What are you going to do to stop me?"

Her attention moves to Scarlett. "How can you be with a man like him?"

Scarlett shakes her head. "He's a better man than you think. No matter what he did to you, your husband was going to do the same to me."

I feel a sense of pride that Scarlett would stick up for me like that. Although, I'm not a better man than Aida thinks. I'm a savage, and nothing has changed.

Aida nods. "I don't doubt that." She glances over the other side of the casino, looking torn. She meets my gaze. "Despite what you did to me, I don't want any bloodshed here." She steps out of our way. "Now get out before he spots you."

Scarlett smiles at Aida. "Thank you."

Aida shakes her head. "Go, now."

I drag her to the exit and open the door. The moment we're out on the sidewalk, I can relax slightly.

"That was too close," Scarlett says, looking as relieved as I feel.

"We're not out of the woods yet, darlin'," I say,

leading her toward the parking lot around the corner. "We need to be fast before they decide to search outside of the casino." I lead her around the corner, only to pull her straight back around it fast.

"Fuck," I growl, irritated that three of Milo's men are guarding my Chevy Impala. "That Italian son of a bitch is about to rob me of another one of my favorite cars."

Scarlett's brow furrows. "Another?"

I remember the moment I heard the explosion outside of my house, running out to find my most beloved possession scattered all over my drive. "He blew up my 1967 L88 Corvette Convertible. It's the reason I took his wife."

Scarlett's eyes widen. "Wow, that must have hurt."

I can feel the dangerous rage inside of me as I remember it, but it was nothing compared to seeing Milo's hands on Scarlett. "It hurt, but not as much as it hurt when I saw him hold that knife to your neck."

Scarlett searches my eyes. "What are you saying?"

My stomach twists nervously. "I'm saying that you are everything to me, baby girl, now we need to find a cab." I tighten my grip on her hand, pulling her the opposite way to the parking lot.

The street outside the casino's main entrance is busy, but men are searching the crowd for us. "We're in the fucking lion's den now, darlin'." I pull Scarlett to a stop at a crossing, waiting to get over to the other side of the road. We don't exactly blend in with the clothes we're wearing.

"They're going to see us," Scarlett murmurs.

I shake my head. "They won't if you keep your cool." The lights change, and we walk across the crossing to a rank of cabs.

We find one that has its lights on and get in. "Beacon Hills, lad," I say.

The cab driver nods and turns his light off, pulling out of the rank. As we drive past Milo's men searching in the street, I feel a sense of relief wash over me. "Thank fuck for that," I murmur, setting my hand on Scarlett's thigh. "We made it, baby girl."

She looks into my eyes adoringly. "It looks like we did." She sighs heavily. "What about your car?"

I shrug. "I'll buy a new one if my men can't collect it later." I tighten my grip on her thigh. "The main thing is we're both safe." I kiss her passionately.

She nods in response and settles back in the seat. "I guess it was a bit of a disaster tonight. The war is nowhere near ending?" she asks.

I shake my head. "No, we've got a long road ahead." I can tell the war worries her. It's not surprising, considering she's carrying my baby.

Another weakness that Milo can exploit once he finds out unless we ensure he doesn't.

"What happens now?" she asks, looking at me expectantly.

I swallow hard, knowing that it's about time I put

my heart on the line. Scarlett is everything to me, and so is our baby. Sure, I'm not cut out to be a father, but Scarlett will make an excellent mother. Somehow, we'll work this out.

"I want you to stay with me, not because I bought you or I made you stay." I search her brilliant blue eyes. "I want you to stay because you want to." My chest aches at the words I'm about to say. "If you don't want to, then I understand if you leave."

She shakes her head. "I want to stay. It's crazy considering the way we met, but I want to."

I smile at her and kiss her lips, letting my tongue search every inch of her mouth. When we break apart, we're breathless. "I love you, Scarlett," I murmur, barely above a whisper.

"I love you too."

My heart expands in my chest hearing her say those three words to me. Three words I didn't believe anyone would ever say, other than my sister.

The darkness that rules me is easing every moment I spend with my baby girl. "I can't wait to get you home and do so many dirty things to you."

She shivers against me, clenching her thighs together. "What kind of dirty things, daddy?" she whispers, making me harder than a rock.

I groan as I move my lips to her ear. "You're going to have to be a good girl and wait and see."

She pouts at me. "Can't you tell me?"

I shake my head. "Don't push me, or I'll be

punishing you too." It's impossible not to notice the way her eyes light up at the mention of punishment.

"What if I enjoy being punished?" she asks.

I tighten my grip on her thigh, hard enough to hurt. "You're such a naughty girl." I notice the cab driver glancing at us in the rearview mirror. "Careful, it looks like we have ourselves an audience again."

Scarlett glances at the cab driver, and he turns his attention back to the road.

I pull my cell phone out of my pocket. "I need to contact Niall and tell him to go back for my car when the heat dies down."

Scarlett nods and watches as I type out my message to him.

Niall types back fast.

Will do, boss. Also, Darragh confirmed it's done. He said you'd know what he meant.

My heart skips a beat as I glance over at Scarlett. "By the way, baby girl. I promised your father wouldn't be able to hurt anyone again, and he won't."

Scarlett's brow furrows. "What did you do?"

I shake my head. "Nothing, just pulled some strings in the jail." I reach for her and pull her close. "He's gone forever and won't be able to hurt you or anyone ever again."

Tears flood down her cheeks as she holds onto me tightly. "Thank you, Malachy, for everything," she murmurs as we fall into silence, holding each other.

The journey takes forever, but finally, he pulls

through the gates of my home. I get out of the cab and help Scarlett out before paying the cab driver.

Scarlett still looks as beautiful as ever, despite the crazy ordeal we went through. She's tough and can withstand the shit my life will throw at her.

I slide my hand onto the small of her back and guide her toward the house. "Are you hungry, darlin'?"

Scarlett shakes her head, cheeks flushing. "Not for food."

I growl, feeling the savage and primal side of me coming out in full force. "If you're suggesting you are hungry for my cock, baby girl, then tell me."

She bites her bottom lip. "I'm hungry for your cock, daddy," she says, teasing me.

I lift her off her feet, making her squeal in surprise.

"What are you doing?" she asks.

I don't answer her and carry her up the stairs toward the bedroom. When I get to the door, I twist the handle and kick it open. I shut it with my foot, carrying Scarlett still.

Once I get her to my room, I set her down in front of the mirror on the wall. "I'm going to strip you." I set my hand on the clasp of her necklace and undo it, placing it gently down on the chair. Next, I unzip her dress and gently peel the fabric away from her luscious body. "You are perfect," I murmur, kissing her shoulder.

She shivers. "I need you inside of me," she says, making my cock harder than I believed possible.

"Patience, baby girl." I set the dress down over the

back of the chair. "I'm going to take my time with you tonight." I lift her into my arms and carry her to the bed, gently setting her down. "We have all the time in the world, darlin'." I kiss her lips passionately. "I want to prove to you how much I love you."

The statement hangs in the air between us as I stare into her brilliant blue eyes. Love wasn't in the cards for me. At least, I didn't think it was.

Then Scarlett came blazing into my life and caught me off guard. Even if I don't deserve her, she's mine forever.

29

SCARLETT

*M*alachy clips my ankles into the restraints fitted to his bed before clamping my wrists in too.

I can't believe how lucky I am that he loves me back, even if he is dark and twisted. It feels like perhaps we can both heal each other's wounds.

Wounds that people we should have been able to trust in our lives inflicted on us.

He runs a finger through my dripping wet pussy. "You are so wet," he growls before plunging his tongue inside of me.

I moan as he devours me, plunging his tongue as deep as possible. He grazes the tip of his teeth over my clit, making the pleasure increase threefold.

My heart skips a beat as he sinks his teeth into my thigh, biting me hard enough to hurt. "Malachy," I cry, feeling my pleasure spike.

He groans against my skin. "I can't ever get enough of you crying my name." He slides three fingers deep inside of me, continuing to lick and bite my thighs.

There was no way I'd ever believe I'd enjoy pain during sex. It's an odd sensation, but one I can't get enough of.

Malachy continues to push me toward the edge, plunging his finger in and out of me, hard and fast. Every time I think I'm about to come, he backs off.

"Please, daddy, I need to come," I whine.

Malachy smirks against my skin. "Not yet." His fingers leave me, and I watch as he licks them clean. "So sweet, baby girl."

I watch as he spins the shackles around on the bed. "On all fours, now," he orders.

I do as he says in a heartbeat, eager to please him. I watch him rummage in the nightstand and pull out his flogger.

"Time for your punishment," he murmurs, lightly brushing the leather strips over my ass.

My thighs quiver, feeling the anticipation building inside of me. "Please, daddy," I beg.

He brings the flogger down hard on my right cheek, making me yelp. "You're my dirty little slut, begging me to whip you, baby girl."

I love it when he calls me his slut, as I am a slut for him. It's crazy the way he's turned me into this. All of my reservations are gone when I'm with him because I trust him.

He flogs me until my ass is stinging. Then he gently licks my asshole.

At first, I tense as it's such a dirty thing to do.

"Relax, darlin'," he murmurs, before continuing to lick my ass. He thrusts a finger in and out of my pussy increasing the pleasure in ways I can hardly explain.

He keeps licking me, making me feel better than I've felt before. I can hear him unbuckling his pants, which makes the excitement increase. My pussy is aching for his cock.

Suddenly, he thrusts his cock deep inside of me. There's no warning as he starts to fuck me roughly, spanking my ass with his hand. "Fuck, that tight little cunt is heaven," he growls.

I can feel myself nearing the edge almost instantly. "Yes, daddy, I'm going to come," I cry.

He growls behind me like an animal, continuing to fuck me right through my orgasm. He doesn't stop as stars explode behind my eyes and my thighs give way.

Heat sets my body on fire, searing my nerves. I can hardly see for a moment, wondering if I've died and gone to heaven. All the time, Malachy continues to pound into me, rough and fast.

My pussy spasms with pleasure as he builds that amazing sensation inside of me again.

"That's it, baby girl, take my cock," he grunts.

He grabs hold of my throat from behind, forcing me to arch my back. Malachy leans over and speaks into my ear, "You're my dirty little girl, and I'm going to use you any way I please."

"Yes, daddy," I cry, "Please, use me."

He bites the back of my neck before pulling his cock out and leaving me empty.

"What are you—"

My question earns me a sharp spank on my ass. "No questions." He grabs a bottle of lube out of the nightstand, making me instantly anxious. "I want to fuck your pretty little asshole," he murmurs, making me tense at the thought.

"Won't that hurt, daddy?" I ask.

"On your back," he orders, spinning the shackles around so I can move. When our eyes meet, he shakes his head. "Don't worry. I'll go slow."

I swallow hard as I look into his emerald green eyes. There's no doubt that I trust this man, but the thought of his huge cock in such a tight, small hole makes me nervous.

He covers his fingers in lube before putting some on my ass. Slowly, he slides a finger inside of me.

The sensation is strange at first and stings a little. As Malachy slowly thrusts his finger in and out, the pleasure increases. "Oh, wow," I murmur, surprised to find I enjoy it.

Malachy takes his time, slowly stretching me. Next with two fingers, then three, until he has all four inside me, and I'm moaning like a whore.

"Oh, yes," I cry, feeling myself getting close again. "Fuck my ass, daddy," I beg, desperate to feel him inside such a forbidden, dirty place.

He smiles down at me. "Such a dirty girl, begging for my cock in your ass."

I watch him as he squirts lube all over his cock before adding more to my stretched virgin hole. "I can't wait to fuck your tight, virgin ass." He kisses my lips, making me moan into his mouth.

"Fuck my ass, please, daddy," I beg, knowing how much he loves it.

He slides his fingers gently around my throat. "You are perfect," he murmurs before pressing the head of his thick cock against my hole.

I relax, looking into his eyes.

He slides the head of his cock into my ass before pushing every inch inside of me. The prior stretching helps, and at first, it just stings a little.

"Damn, that's tight," he growls.

I love the way he sounds so out of control. Slowly, he moves in and out of my ass, allowing me a chance to get used to it.

"You're practically pulling me inside," he growls, as I see the desire sparking in his eyes. "So fucking good," he grunts.

Before long, he's fucking my ass hard and rough. I'm surprised at how good it feels, my pussy dripping everywhere as he takes my anal virginity.

"How does it feel to have my cock inside your ass?" he asks, biting my bottom lip.

"Amazing, daddy," I reply, moaning as he increases the speed.

"Good girl, I want to feel you come while I'm deep inside this tight little ass of yours." He bites my collarbone, moving in and out of me at a steady tempo. "Then, I'm going to fill your ass to the brim with cum and plug it, so you have it inside of you all damn night," he growls.

The thought only heightens my pleasure. "Yes, daddy, I want your cum in my ass," I moan, feeling my nipples get so hard they hurt.

He growls as he fucks me harder, rubbing my clit as he does.

My mind goes blank as I watch my beautiful savage of a man fucking me, his eyes wild and frantic. My pussy gushes as I come apart, and my muscles spasm.

Malachy roars like a majestic beast. "That's it, baby girl. Come with my cock deep in your ass," he growls, pumping a few more times before shooting his hot cum deep inside of me.

My vision blurs and turns white as he sets me on fire. Every nerve ending in my body lights up as he continues to pump in and out of my ass, fucking me through it.

Once he's drained every drop of cum inside of me, he reaches into the nightstand and pulls out a butt plug.

"I'm going to make sure it can't come out, okay?" he asks.

I bite my bottom lip. "Okay, daddy."

He groans and slowly slips his enormous cock out of my ass before squirting lube on the plug and slipping it inside of me instead. "Now, you can sleep with my cum in your ass," he murmurs, kissing me gently.

I watch him as he unshackles me before lying down by my side.

"Come here, darlin'." He beckons for me to rest my head on his chest.

I do as he says, placing a hand on his chiseled, tattooed stomach. "That was amazing," I say, shaking my head. "I never thought anal would feel like that."

He chuckles. "Had you ever thought about having anal sex?" he asks.

"No, I thought it would hurt like hell," I say.

He sighs, resting his head back. "You are an angel, darlin'."

I laugh. "After what we just did, I'd say angel isn't right."

He looks down at me, smiling. "Probably not. You're a dirty little sex demon instead, is that better?"

I smile and nod. "Sounds about right."

"What am I then?" he asks.

"The devil who corrupted me."

He nods in response. "Sounds about right."

We lie in comfortable silence, holding each other. I'm certain that I've never been happier in my life.

When I went to that auction, the last thing I expected to find was love. I'll be forever grateful that I sold myself to Malachy, as it's the best decision I ever made.

30

EPILOGUE

SCARLETT

*M*y heart is pounding as I stare out onto the stage.

This is the moment I've been waiting for. A chance at the career I've always dreamed of. The dancer before me is finishing her piece, and I'm on next. There are major critics from the industry here for the show.

As her music dies down, my music starts, and the lady walks off stage. "Good luck," she says as she walks past me.

I feel the adrenaline increase as I step out onto the stage. The ballet company that agreed to give me a shot is prestigious, and this could make or break my dance career before it's started.

I notice Malachy at the front of the crowd, and instantly my worries fade away. He smiles up at me, and it feels like everyone else fades into the background.

My mom sits by his side, beaming proudly, with

Frank sitting next to her. I'm so thankful I could save her life. She's now been free from cancer for over six months. Frank asked her to marry him, and they are happily settled in a lovely apartment we bought for them.

She never learned the extent of my lies, since my relationship with Malachy became my cover. All she believes is that my husband is very wealthy, and that's how I could afford the apartment. She doesn't know that I sold my virginity to Malachy and never will.

Alicia was a little disappointed she couldn't come too, but she got the job of watching baby Liam tonight as well as her own baby, Aiden. Malachy and Alicia have had a crazy year full of tension since he learned the truth about the man I saw her kissing, but I know deep down he's happy for her. However, that's another story entirely.

I twist into my first moves, rising onto my toes, and elegantly pirouette across the stage. Once on the other side, I assemblé back to the center of the stage, keeping time with the music. My heart is pounding so hard it makes it difficult to focus on the music, but I try to ignore it.

I transition into the arabesque before moving back into a pirouette. The lights beaming onto the stage are hotter than ever before, but I think it's because of the pressure. The music slows, and so do my moves, moving into an adage as I glide on the center of the stage.

All the while, I can feel the thousands of eyes on me from the crowd.

I finish up strongly as the tempo increases, finishing with three grande jetés and a plié.

The clapping is a welcome sound. I feel my heart rate even out when the dance is over, bowing to the crowd. Once the music cuts off and the next song starts, I get off the stage quickly to make way for the next dancer.

I'm almost thankful it's over, which is strange as I normally love dancing, even in front of a crowd. The area behind the curtain is quiet, as I was one of the last to perform.

My heart skips a beat when a pair of arms wrap around my waist. "You were amazing, baby girl," Malachy murmurs into my ear. "A real princess up on that stage."

I feel the press of his hard cock against my ass. Even here, he's insatiable. "Did you leave my mom in the crowd?" I ask.

"Don't worry, she's with Frank." He smiles against my neck. "Did you enjoy your performance?"

I shake my head. "Not really. I was so nervous."

Malachy spins me to face him. "I thought this was your dream?"

I nod. "It is, but the pressure is going to take some getting used to."

He smiles at me. "You will get the hang of it. I

could hear the critic behind me getting very excited by your pirouette, whatever the fuck that is."

I laugh. "I'll have to teach you all the different moves."

Malachy's eyes widen. "Nah, I think I'll stick with boxing, baby girl." He kisses my cheek. "No offense."

He glances up above the stage. "How about we sneak upstairs and have fun?"

I swallow hard, glancing around. "That could end my career if we got caught, Malachy."

He leans closer. "Don't worry. We won't get caught."

I feel the need come to life between my thighs. "Okay, daddy," I reply.

He smirks at me using that word and takes my hand, leading me up the stairs to the top grid above the stage and fly tower. There's no one up here, but it feels unbelievably wrong to consider fucking here.

"Are you sure this is a—"

Malachy silences me with his mouth, plundering mine with his tongue frantically. "I've always wanted to fuck a ballerina," he murmurs teasingly. "I think it's the tutu that's so sexy."

"Is that right, daddy?" I ask.

He growls softly. "Yes, baby girl." He lifts me and carries me, pushing my back against the wall.

I moan as he kisses my neck and lifts the skirt of my tutu.

He pops open the leotard I'm wearing and rips a

hole in my tights, making me gasp. "Do you have to destroy my clothes?"

He bites my collarbone. "It's the only way to get my cock inside you," he growls, making my thighs quiver. "Is the butt plug still in?" he asks.

My thighs quiver as I remember the plug he stuck inside of me before we left, after he filled my ass with cum. "Of course, daddy."

He groans. "I bet you can't wait to be filled in both holes, can you, darlin'?"

I shake my head. "No, I can't wait."

I hear him fumble with his pants, and before I know it, he thrusts into me hard. No warning, no warm-up. He always knows I'm ready whenever he wants me. My pussy is instantly wet the moment he kisses my lips.

The sensation of his cock pressing against the thick plug in my ass is amazing. I groan as he fucks me like a savage against the wall.

Malachy places a hand over my mouth, making sure I don't make too much noise. "Careful, baby girl. You don't want everyone to know what a naughty little ballerina you are." He bites my lip. "So naughty that you danced with a butt plug in your ass in front of all those people."

I shudder at the thought of being caught as he moves inside of me. It's crazy that it's a year and a half on, and I'm still as desperate as ever for him. Our desire for one another has only grown.

We've talked about having another baby, but it

would mean putting my dancing career on hold. It might be the end of it if we have another baby soon. I can't help but feel that I'd be okay with that. My passion is dancing, which will never change, but building a family with Malachy would be worth the sacrifice.

He bites my bottom lip, sending a thrilling pain through my core. "You are fucking perfect, my little ballerina," he murmurs, continuing to fuck me hard against the wall.

"Yes, daddy, fuck me like that," I cry, feeling the pressure inside of me mounting.

He groans. "You are so wet, darlin'. Always so fucking wet for me."

I rest my head back against the wall, keeping my arms locked around his neck. The full sensation of the butt plug in my ass, along with his huge cock in my pussy is enough to tip me over the edge, but I hold on.

"Good girl. I know you want to come, but you need to wait until I tell you," he says, grunting as he picks up the pace.

"Yes, daddy. It's hard, but I'm holding on," I reply, knowing how much it drives him crazy when I obey.

He kisses me passionately, tongue tangling with mine as he does. "You're such a good girl, Scarlett," he says once he breaks the kiss. "Now come for me so I can fill you with my cum," he murmurs against my lips. "I want both of your holes full of my seed."

His dirty talk is all it takes as I come undone, screaming so loud that I'm sure people will hear me.

Malachy is quick to stifle the sound with his lips, grunting as he tumbles over the edge too.

I feel him emptying his cum deep inside of my pussy, making me his little slut for the second time tonight. It's crazy that our desire for each other knows no bounds.

We rest for a moment in the same position, panting for air.

He pulls his cock out of me and lowers me to my feet. "Damn, baby girl, that was hot," he says, kissing me again with such passion. "I think your mom and Frank will probably wonder where the fuck we are, though."

The mention of my mom snaps me out of my lust-filled daze. "Shit, we best go." I clench my thighs together. "Although now you ripped my tights, your cum is already dripping through the fabric."

Malachy smiles at me. "Good, everyone should see what my dirty little girl has been up to."

I shake my head. "That's not funny. Can you tell?" I ask.

Malachy looks at my tights before shaking his head. "No, darlin'. I promise."

We head down the steps and sneak out of the stage area into the lobby. Malachy keeps a powerful arm around my back as he guides me toward the exit.

My mom smiles when she sees us, rushing over to hug me. "You were amazing, sweetheart," she says.

Frank nods. "You were great, Scarlett."

I smile at her and Frank, knowing she has to say that because she's my mom. "Thank you." I glance around, noticing the place is pretty empty now. "What time is it?" I ask.

My mom glances at her watch. "It's nine o'clock."

I can feel the heat filtering through my body as Malachy's cum slowly drips down my tights. "Shall we get going, then?" I ask, desperate to get the hell out of here. "Alicia will want to get off babysitting duties, I'm sure."

My mom looks a little disappointed. "Oh, I thought we might have all gone for some dinner." She waves her hand. "Of course, you two get home to Liam and tell him I'll see him for lunch tomorrow."

I smile and hug my mom again. "Sure, see you tomorrow."

Malachy shakes Frank's hand and hugs my mom. I'm surprised how well she has got on with Malachy ever since they met. We wave them off as they head into town to get something to eat before returning to the parking lot.

I head to my side of the Chevy Impala, which Malachy's men recovered on Milo's casino night. Malachy closes me in against it. He nips my ear. "Such a dirty little girl with my cum dripping down your tights, aren't you?" he asks.

I shiver, knowing that tonight is going to be a long night. We're both insatiable and ready for so much more. "Yes, daddy. I'm your dirty little girl."

He growls softly and spins me around, kissing my lips passionately. "I love you, baby girl."

I look into his gleaming emerald eyes. "I love you too."

He smirks. "Now bend over the hood so I can fuck you right here and now," he orders.

I glance around, making sure there's no one else in the parking lot. Not that it would be the first time we'd been seen fucking in public.

I push off the car and bend over the hood, glancing over my shoulder at him. "Okay, daddy," I say, watching the way his eyes light up. They move between my plugged asshole and dripping pussy filled with cum.

Our love is dirty and raw, but it's real as it gets. I never thought I'd fall in love, but I'm lucky I found my knight in shining armor in the most unlikely place.

THANK you for reading Savage Daddy, the second book in the Boston Mafia Doms Series. I hope that you enjoyed reading Malachy and Scarlett's story.

The next book in this series follows Sicilian Don Fabio Alteri and Gia's story in the third book of the series, Ruthless Daddy. This book is available through Kindle Unlimited or to buy on Amazon.

Ruthless Daddy: A Dark Forbidden Mafia Romance

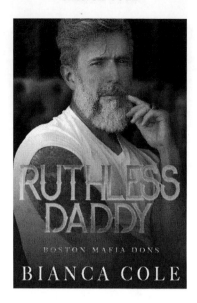

I ignored Aida's warnings, and now I'm ensnared in a ruthless man's trap.

When I went to give Fabio Alteri a piece of my mind, I never expected the visit to take a forbidden turn. Aida told me not to go but in a drunken fury I visited the dangerous don. Angry that this man would tear my friend from me the way he did—his own daughter.

Then, our eyes met and it felt like he set my soul on fire. I shouldn't want the ruthless Sicilian mafia don.

He's dangerous.

He's forbidden.

He's got no soul.

And yet, I find myself inexplicably drawn to him. He's broken, and I've always had a tendency to try to fix people. The question is will I be able to fix him, or will he break me instead?

Ruthless Daddy is the third book in the Boston Mafia Doms Series by Bianca Cole. This book is a safe story with no cliffhangers and a happily ever after ending. However, this story has dark themes, hot scenes, violence, content some readers may find upsetting, and bad language. It features an over the top, twisted and possessive Italian crime boss.

ALSO BY BIANCA COLE

The Syndicate Academy

Corrupt Educator: A Dark Forbidden Mafia Academy Romance

Cruel Bully: A Dark Mafia Academy Romance

Chicago Mafia Dons

Merciless Defender: A Dark Forbidden Mafia Romance

Violent Leader: A Dark Enemies to Lovers Captive Mafia Romance

Evil Prince: A Dark Arranged Marriage Romance

Brutal Daddy: A Dark Captive Mafia Romance

Cruel Vows: A Dark Forced Marriage Mafia Romance

Dirty Secret: A Dark Enemies to Loves Mafia Romance

Dark Crown: A Dark Arranged Marriage Romance

Boston Mafia Dons Series

Cruel Daddy: A Dark Mafia Arranged Marriage Romance

Savage Daddy: A Dark Captive Mafia Roamnce

Ruthless Daddy: A Dark Forbidden Mafia Romance

Vicious Daddy: A Dark Brother's Best Friend Mafia Romance

Wicked Daddy: A Dark Captive Mafia Romance

New York Mafia Doms Series

Her Irish Daddy: A Dark Mafia Romance

Her Russian Daddy: A Dark Mafia Romance

Her Italian Daddy: A Dark Mafia Romance

Her Cartel Daddy: A Dark Mafia Romance

Romano Mafia Brother's Series

Her Mafia Daddy: A Dark Daddy Romance

Her Mafia Boss: A Dark Romance

Her Mafia King: A Dark Romance

Bratva Brotherhood Series

Bought by the Bratva: A Dark Mafia Romance

Captured by the Bratva: A Dark Mafia Romance

Claimed by the Bratva: A Dark Mafia Romance

Bound by the Bratva: A Dark Mafia Romance

Taken by the Bratva: A Dark Mafia Romance

Wynton Series

Filthy Boss: A Forbidden Office Romance

Filthy Professor: A First Time Professor And Student
Romance

Filthy Lawyer: A Forbidden Hate to Love Romance

Filthy Doctor: A Fordbidden Romance

Royally Mated Series

Her Faerie King: A Faerie Royalty Paranormal Romance

Her Alpha King: A Royal Wolf Shifter Paranormal
Romance

Her Dragon King: A Dragon Shifter Paranormal Romance

Her Vampire King: A Dark Vampire Romance

ABOUT THE AUTHOR

I love to write stories about over the top alpha bad boys who have heart beneath it all, fiery heroines, and happily-ever-after endings with heart and heat. My stories have twists and turns that will keep you flipping the pages and heat to set your kindle on fire.

For as long as I can remember, I've been a sucker for a good romance story. I've always loved to read. Suddenly, I realized why not combine my love of two things, books and romance?

My love of writing has grown over the past four years and I now publish on Amazon exclusively, weaving stories about dirty mafia bad boys and the women they fall head over heels in love with.

If you enjoyed this book please follow me on Amazon, Bookbub or any of the below social media platforms for alerts when more books are released.

Printed in Great Britain
by Amazon

16114201R00185